CURSE of
the NIGHT WOLF

Also available by Paul Stewart & Chris Riddell:

FERGUS CRANE
CORBY FLOOD
HUGO PEPPER

THE EDGE CHRONICLES
BEYOND THE DEEPWOODS
STORMCHASER
MIDNIGHT OVER SANCTAPHRAX
THE CURSE OF THE GLOAMGLOZER
THE LAST OF THE SKY PIRATES
VOX
FREEGLADER
THE WINTER KNIGHTS
CLASH OF THE SKY GALLEONS

PAUL STEWART & CHRIS RIDDELL

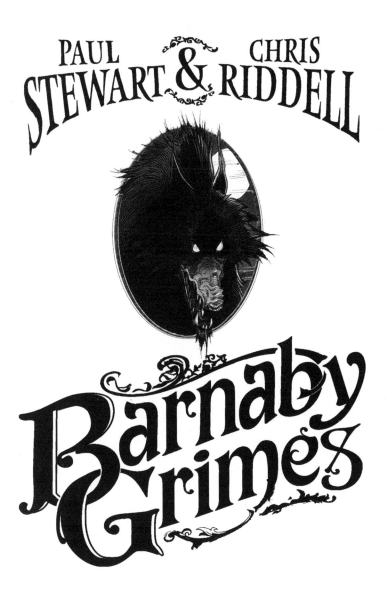

Barnaby Grimes

CURSE of the NIGHT WOLF

Illustrated by Chris Riddell

David Fickling Books

OXFORD · NEW YORK

A DAVID FICKLING BOOK

Published by David Fickling Books
an imprint of Random House Children's Books
a division of Random House, Inc.
New York

Originally published in Great Britain by David Fickling Books,
an imprint of Random House Children's Books, in 2007.

David Fickling Books and colophon are trademarks of David Fickling.

Visit us on the Web! www.randomhouse.com/kids

Educators and librarians, for a variety of teaching tools, visit us at
www.randomhouse.com/teachers

Library of Congress Cataloging-in-Publication Data
Curse of the Night Wolf / Paul Stewart and Chris Riddell. —
1st American ed.
p.   cm.—(Barnaby Grimes)
Summary: Soon after Victorian messenger Barnaby Grimes is attacked
by a huge beast while crossing London's rooftops, he becomes entangled
in a mystery involving patent medicine, impoverished patients,
and very expensive furs.
ISBN 978-0-385-75125-4 (trade) — ISBN 978-0-385-75126-1 (lib. bdg.)
[1. Messengers—Fiction. 2. Patent medicines—Fiction.
3. Physicians—Fiction. 4. Werewolves—Fiction. 5. London
(England)—History—1800–1950—Fiction. 6. Great Britain—History—
Victoria, 1837–1901—Fiction. 7. Mystery and detective stories.]
PZ7.S84975Cur 2008
[Fic]—dc22
2008001697

Printed in the United States of America
September 2008
10 9 8 7 6 5 4 3 2 1

First American Edition

For my nephew, Stephen – P.S.
For Jack – C.R.

CHAPTER 1

*H*ave you ever felt your skin being peeled slowly away from your arms and legs? Your muscles being torn and shredded as every bone in your body fights to burst through your flesh? Have you ever felt every tendon and sinew stretched to breaking point as your skeleton attempts to rip itself apart from the inside?

I have, and I'll never forget it.

I remember moonlight. The great silver disc of the full moon bearing down into my upraised eyes, its intoxicating light seeping into my pores and coursing through my veins, stirring something deep, deep within me.

And then the pain. Terrible convulsions

racked my body, my skin seemed to be on fire and, looking down in horror, I saw my fingers and toes contract into hard, claw-tipped paws. My neck strained, my belly cramped, while the muscles in my chest and shoulders rippled and rolled as though a colony of trapped rats was writhing beneath my skin.

At the back of my throat I felt a burning sensation as the root of my tongue swelled and squirmed, leaving me choking for breath. I coughed, and my tongue leaped out between my parted lips and lolled from the corner of my mouth, down past my chin. Strands of drool splattered onto the floor and glinted in the moonlight.

Such pain I endured. Such terrible pain. It felt as though my very skull had been placed in a carpenter's vice, which was being screwed tighter and tighter.

And then the noises began . . .

There was a creaking, cracking sound inside my ears, and I knew that my jaw was thrusting forward even as my nose did the same. The next moment I realized I could see them both at the same time through my narrowed eyes. I shook my head violently and tried to scream, but all that emerged were growls and yelps that turned into a terrible howl as my terror grew.

I tried to get away, but was overwhelmed with an impossible heaviness that pinned me to the spot. I was trapped, scarcely able to move so much as a muscle – yet my senses were on fire.

My hearing was more acute than ever before. My eyesight had sharpened, so that everything looked bright and clear – though curiously elongated, as if I was looking through a slightly warped lens. My nose quivered with excitement as a thousand different scents and odours assailed it.

There was the pungent smell of linseed oil in the varnished woodwork. There was the fragrant perfume of a recent visitor – as well as the sour underlying sweat she had been attempting to conceal. There was tile polish. Spilled milk. Crushed grass. Pigeon feathers. Soot. Dust. Tarmacadam. A trace of vomit. A hint of dog . . .

And then the itching began. All over my body. Scabrous, overwhelming and impossible to ignore, it had me scraping and scratching at every inch of my skin with my claws, using all the energy I could muster. And as I did so, my jaw dropped with a mixture of horror and shock as I witnessed my smooth, almost hairless skin begin to sprout thick, dark fur.

Horrified, I stared up and howled once more. My clothes lay in tatters about me.

The cramped and dingy chamber was heavily padded. Each wall and surface had been covered with a heavy, pale-grey felt quilting that deadened all sound – quilting which, even as I looked, revealed dried splashes of blood.

Above my head was the skylight – a thick

double-glassed window in the low sloping ceiling, like a monstrous eye – which concentrated the beams of light from the full moon down into the chamber. I stared back, transfixed.

Then I heard it. A low unpleasant chuckle that came from behind me. With great effort, I slowly turned my head . . .

A figure was looking down at me.

He was dressed in heavy robes and a huge, sinister hood which obscured his head and face completely. The moonlight glinted on the dark glass panels that concealed his eyes – and on the huge silver and glass syringe he had clasped in his gloved hand.

I stared back, unable to move so much as a muscle.

The next moment the hideous apparition started moving towards me; slowly, deliberately, the syringe held out before him. I let out a whimper as a spasm of fear convulsed my body.

Thump-thump-thump.

He took another step closer, raising the

The moonlight glinted on the dark glass panels that concealed his eyes…

syringe and letting a couple of drops of silvery-white liquid emerge from the tip of the great needle and trickle down the side. My ears pricked up and my lips drew back in a terrified snarl – I couldn't get away from him. I couldn't move. Another spasm ran down my spine.

Thump-thump-thump.

What *was* that sound? Something thumping on the padded floor, as if beating a rhythm with my pounding heart. The figure raised the needle-sharp syringe as I fought to regain control of my pain-racked body.

Thump-thump-thump.

There it was again. With a jolt, I realized what it was thumping behind me . . .

It was my tail.

CHAPTER 2

I'll never forget the events of that terrible night as long as I live; events that, even now, as I speak of them, bring a cold sweat to my brow and a tremor to my hand. Yet speak of them I must, for in their retelling, perhaps I can offer some insight into the black heart of this great, bustling city.

It is a dark world that I, as a 'tick-tock lad', have come to know all too well. And there are horrors I have witnessed that I wouldn't wish on my worst enemy. One such horror is the subject of this tale . . .

As I said, I'm a tick-tock lad – a sort of cross between a messenger and a delivery boy, only a tick-tock lad has to be faster than the first and twice as sharp as the second. It's no job for a green-willow or a haywain bumpkin, make no mistake.

I know this city like the back of my hand – every alley, every twitten, every street. I have to: it's my trade. Getting about it is second nature to me. Give me any two places and I'll tell you the quickest way to get from one to the other in an instant. Time is money. Tick-tock – the ticking of the clock . . .

That's why they call us tick-tock lads.

You won't find us stuck behind a desk in some poky office. Always out and about, we are. Whether it's witnessing wills or serving writs, recording testimonies or collecting petitions, dispensing subscriptions or running bond certificates, it's all in a day's work for a tick-tock lad. And I've had my fair share of strange assignments, I can tell you.

There was the time I had to deliver a consignment of blue-speckled Muscovy duck eggs, still warm, to the Wetland and Fen Ornithological Society in time for their Annual Hatching Banquet. There was the occasion of Lady Fitzrovia's secret masked ball, when I had to distribute two hundred gold-edged invitations in the middle of the night – and with half the scribblers from the gossip sheets on my trail.

And then there was the time when I was called upon to deliver subscriptions to Colonel Wybridge-Tonks's historical pamphlet, *Chronic Afflictions from the Uncleansed Drain* – and found myself being pursued through the sewers by a pack of flesh-eating salamanders . . .

But that is a story so gruesome it deserves a book of its own.

The terrible dark evil of my current tale began with the seemingly innocent fashion for fur collars and cuffs, known as the Westphalian trim. It was all the rage a while back – but then fashion is a strange thing.

One week you can't move down Gallop Row for raffish swells in double-hoop top hats. The next, they've moved on to straw tom-o'tassels, just like that. And those fine young ladies who promenade along High Market and Regency Mall are just as fickle. One season it's all fingerless lace gloves and sealskin boots, the next, oriental skirts and lapdogs the size of dormice.

As for me, a twelve-pocket poacher's waist-coat, a coalstack hat and a trusty swordstick are all I need, but then I've never been a follower of fashion. No, I leave that to the swells and fine ladies. And as for them, well, they couldn't seem to get enough of this Westphalian trim.

The fur was thick and soft and luxurious, but what truly set it apart from your average rabbit or squirrel fur – or stray cat, for that matter – was its lustre. It was a lustre that had to be seen to be believed; a lustre so exquisite that the fur itself seemed almost to glow.

They couldn't seem to get enough of this Westphalian trim.

The story went that it was made from the pelt of the great night wolf – a rare species that roamed the forests around the remote mountain town of Tannenburg in the East. The skins of these rare beasts were reputedly so valuable that the merest sliver used on a collar or cuff would enhance the value of a well-tailored jacket or coat a thousandfold.

It wasn't long before the swells and fine ladies of Gallop Row and Regency Mall were competing with each other for the highest collar and most generous cuff finished off in the exquisite Westphalian trim. As I say, it was the fashion, and I would have thought no more about it had it not been for the grim adventure that was about to befall me late one damp spring afternoon as I set off towards the austere legal offices of Bradstock and Clink.

Young Bradley Bradstock and old Aloysius Clink were regular clients. I had picked up a batch of summonses from the two lawyers as usual and delivered them, before returning to their offices in my usual way. A normal job on a normal day – or so I thought.

I couldn't have been more wrong.

Nothing could have prepared me for the sight that met my eyes up on the old chamber roofs as I took my usual short cut. It was a sight that made my blood run cold . . .

CHAPTER 3

But to understand the true horror of the terrible events that began that night, I must tell you of my friend, Old Benjamin.

Old Benjamin had lived in a pair of dingy rooms in that tall, wedge-shaped building on the corner of Water Lane and Black Dog Alley for as far back as I could remember. Drove a city coach-and-four for years, as I recall. 'Course, with his wrinkled face and shock of unruly hair, he'd always seemed old to me – but then I suppose all kids think that adults look old, don't they?

Anyway, when I was a nipper, I used to see him out front on his days off. He'd drag a battered old coachman's chair onto the pavement at all hours of the day or night, and sit there watching the world go by.

Sometimes he was in a good mood, and would greet passers-by, having a laugh and a joke with anyone who would stop for a chat. Other times, he'd be as miserable as a deacon's dog on Friday, cursing the drayman's nag for the piles of steaming manure left on the cobbles, berating the street urchins for throwing rotten oranges at windows, and shaking his fist at the wealthy toffs and swells for not tipping their hats as they hurried past.

I've got to say, though, he was always all right with me. More often than not, he'd catch me when I was passing on some errand or other, and get me to carry out a little errand of his own – taking a message to one of his coachman colleagues on the other side of town or bringing him something back from the shops. Then he'd flip me a coin as a reward – something small, but enough for a gobstopper or a sherbet dab . . .

And if ever he noticed me walking when he was driving his city coach-and-four, then he'd stop and let me ride up top for free.

I used to love that coach of his. It was smaller than the ones you get nowadays. There was no staircase up to the top deck, just rungs at the back. And when you'd climbed up, you had to sit back to back with the others already there, on a narrow bench – the knife-board, Old Benjamin used to call it – which ran along the middle of the roof. There was nothing to hold on to and no protection from the weather. All us passengers up there would cling to one another for dear life every time we went round a corner, shrieking with fear and laughter . . .

Yes, Old Benjamin was a good friend to me. Later on, of course, he'd been forced to retire by 'coachman's lung' – a dry hacking cough caused by stable dust and sooty street air – and after that he spent most of his time in that coachman's chair of his.

That was where I saw him one bright, sunny spring day as I was passing on some errand or other. He was looking tired and ill, with dark rings beneath his watery blue eyes, and his thick shock of pewter-grey hair uncombed.

'Barnaby,' he said as he saw me approaching. His lips peeled back in a smile to reveal stained, gappy teeth. 'Barnaby Grimes, you young whippersnapper. Of all people! What brings you— *khaaagh khaaagh—*'

All at once his pleasantries gave way to a fit of coughing. He reached towards me, those watery eyes streaming and his face turning a deep, dark purple as he tried in vain to speak. The hacking cough grew more unpleasant by the moment, gurgling in his throat and rattling in his chest.

'Khaaagh … khaaagh … khaaagh … khaaagh …'

Bulgy-eyed and gasping for breath, he looked as though he was going to drop dead on the spot.

'Khaaagh ... khaaagh ... khaaagh ...'

With flailing arms, he gestured desperately to his back. Doing as I was bid, I stepped forward and thumped the old coachman hard between the shoulders.

To my horror, his coughing grew worse. Then, with a sudden wheeze, he abruptly fell still. His head lolled down onto his chest.

'Are ... are you all right?' I asked nervously.

He looked up, his face drained of all colour. 'Me coachman's lung, it's getting worse ... and worse,' he gasped, shaking his head miserably as he struggled with the words.

'You should see a doctor about it,' I suggested.

'Doctors! Don't talk to me about doctors!' said Old Benjamin, suddenly agitated. 'They look at you for two minutes, use a lot of fancy-sounding words, then suggest you take a rest-cure in the mountains or on the coast. And charge you the earth for the privilege. Pah!' He shook his head in disgust. 'No, what I need, young Barnaby, is a good old-fashioned cure-all – a cordial or some such to pick me up. You know the sort of thing . . .'

I knew just what he meant all right. There were dozens of quack patent medicines on the market. The only trouble was that half of them were highly likely to do more harm than good, which was why so few of them stayed on sale for long.

Dr Jolyon's Fever Powder, for instance, was removed from the shelves when it was found to raise rather than lower a patient's temperature; Morrison's Patent Iron Pills were discontinued when those who took them turned rust-brown; while Godfrey's Cordial was considered by many to be the most likely cause of a whole spate of grisly 'leaking' deaths in the East End of the city.

One of the most popular medicaments around a while ago was Old Mother Berkeley's Patent Tonic. Despite its inventor's claims that it 'can be taken under all circumstances, requiring neither special diet nor confinement to bed', and that 'its timely assistance inevitably cures all complaints and cheers the heart under any misfortune', I reckon the best that could be said for it was that its side effects weren't permanent. True, all your hair fell out – which could be traumatic – but it usually grew back again.

Anyway, I told Old Benjamin I'd look out for something that might help him, and set off. I was just turning into Mission Lane when I heard his terrible hacking cough echoing down the street after me. It would have to be a miracle cure, I remember thinking to myself, judging from the state of Old Benjamin's lungs.

To my shame, I have to confess that I forgot all about Old Benjamin and his cough almost immediately after that. I'd had a lot on my plate around that time – several new clients with a whole array of problems, ranging from some minor unpleasantness concerning a costermonger's noisy parrot to a tick-tock lads' dispute over the ticket trade at the Easter races which threatened to turn nasty. Then, of course, there was that macabre business I got embroiled in with the haunted marionette theatre . . .

Suffice it to say that when I next bumped into Old Benjamin three or four weeks later, on that fateful day when I'd just finished delivering summonses and was returning to the offices of Bradstock and Clink, the moment our eyes met, I was overwhelmed with guilt. It was getting dark, but he was still outside, sitting in that old coachman's chair.

'Well, well, well,' he exclaimed. 'Look who's turned up again like a bad penny!'

He stuck out his hand in greeting.

'Benjamin,' I said. We shook hands warmly. 'I haven't forgotten about your medicine,' I lied. 'I've just been too busy to check out any cordials or tinctures—'

'No need,' said Old Benjamin cheerily. 'I've found something. Got talking to a passer-by a few weeks ago. He stopped and admired my fine head of hair. I thanked him and explained how it had grown back once I stopped taking Old Mother Berkeley's Patent Tonic. He smiled at that, and when I began coughing, he recommended this . . .'

Old Benjamin reached into his jacket pocket and pulled out a blue glass bottle with a black and silver label on it. He looked down and frowned, then cleared his throat.

'*Doctor Cadwallader's Cordial,*' he read out. 'It's a miracle! My cough has completely gone and I've never felt better in my life.' He returned his attention to the label. '*An efficacious elixir for the enhancement of mental and physical powers . . .'* He looked up, a gappy grin on his face. 'I'll tell you what, Barnaby,' he added. 'It's even improved my eyesight!'

He pulled out the stopper, cleaned round the top of the neck with the palm of his hand and held the bottle out to me. 'Fancy a swig?' he said. 'It's a real tonic.'

'That's very kind of you,' I said, 'but no.' I chuckled. 'I'm feeling fine.'

I didn't add that, even if I did have some ailment, there was nothing on this earth that would tempt me to drink some quack's concoction. I glanced at the label before handing it back: *Dr Theopholus Cadwallader: 27 Hartley Square . . .*

Hartley Square! The place was famously opulent, with great marble-stepped mansions forming a square around an exclusive park. Those who resided there were the richest, choicest and most well-connected medical practitioners in the entire city. Most had made fortunes tending to the ailments – real or imaginary – of the wealthy; few ever ministering to the very real illnesses that ravaged the poorer quarters of the city.

Perhaps this doctor was the exception to prove the rule; perhaps he had taken pity on Old Benjamin. Why else would he have given him a cordial that, by the look of it, was far too expensive for an old coachman to afford?

Then again, it wasn't unheard of for the less reputable practitioners to test their patent potions on the poor and desperate in case of side effects. But perhaps I was being uncharitable.

I examined Old Benjamin more closely. There was colour in his cheeks and a twinkle in his eye. In fact, he looked like a new man. Certainly his cough had cleared up. Maybe he had struck lucky – and if that was the case, then good luck to him, I thought as I tipped my hat and set off again for the offices of Bradstock and Clink to get paid for my day's work.

It had been raining earlier that day, I remember, and the cobbles and tiles were more slippery than usual – not that the rain had done anything to dispel the pall of pale-brown smoke that always hung over the city. I headed down Turbot Alley, swordstick tucked under my arm, over the wall of Davis's ironworks, across the yard on the other side, before shinning up a rusty drain-pipe at the far end and hoisting myself up onto the roof.

As I eased myself up over the guttering and onto the tiles – disturbing a small flock of chattering sparrows as I did so – I found myself grinning involuntarily. Truth be told, this was when I was happiest – high above the city streets, clambering over the rooftops from chimney stack to chimney stack.

Highstacking, it's called – and it's not for the faint-hearted. A tick-tock lad called Tom

Flint taught me to highstack when I was first getting started. Good old Tom . . . A couple of years older than me, he was the best high-stacker in the business – until he broke his neck in Coneyhope Lane. Hugh Shovel crippled himself shortly afterwards, and Shorty Clough fell and drowned in the Union Canal. There aren't many of us high-stackers left any more. Still, I didn't let that bother me that night, up on the rooftops, as I highstacked above the city, leaping from gutter to gable, pillar to pediment – roof to roof – with the arrogant agility of a courting tomcat.

The full moon had already risen and I was heading south-west, orientating myself through the shadows first by the needle-like spire of Pargeter's Mutual Bank, then by the tall, soot-stained brick chimney of Greville's glue works. Not that I gave either of them too much thought. Having come this way dozens of times before, the route – like so many

Leaping from gutter to gable…with the arrogant agility of a courting tomcat.

others that crisscrossed the city – was absolutely familiar. As I made my way across the patchwork of rooftops, it was the week ahead that was uppermost in my thoughts.

I remembered Professor Pinkerton-Barnes and the research into the behaviour of bullfinches that he'd asked me to help him with. I mulled over a request I'd had to deliver a consignment of vipers to the Blackchapel Herpetological Society – they'd be dangerously active if the weather got any warmer. And I made a mental note to return the library books on Mayan hieroglyphics I'd borrowed from Underhill's Library for Scholars of the Arcane, or face a hefty fine . . .

Glancing up, I saw the domed turret of Bradstock and Clink's chambers nestling in a soft haze of indigo. The full moon had crept up into the sky behind it. Pigeons flapped through the smoky air, their wings clapping like muted applause.

The huge brick chimney of Greville's factory was to my left now. I could feel the heat radiating from the furnace below; I could smell the rank, sickly odour of the glue being boiled down. The air shimmered.

I was making my way along the parapet that formed the edge of the flat-roofed building, my arms raised to balance myself and taking care not to slip, when I suddenly became aware that something was wrong . . .

The sparrows that had been following my progress abruptly flapped away, cheeping and chirruping as they went. The sky looked unnaturally curdled as dark swirling clouds swept in across the moon, and there was something particularly rancid about the air. All at once, as the wind dropped, I became acutely aware of a movement behind me.

I looked round.

At first, everything seemed to be just the way it should be. Was it my imagination playing tricks? I asked myself. Was the foul smell of the glue getting to me?

But then, just as I was about to continue, I glimpsed something in the shadows that made my heart miss a beat. There *was* something there. No doubt about it. Something large and solid-looking, hunkered down in the shadowy recess at the bottom of the brick wall.

I heard a hiss. Then a low, menacing snarl. And as the clouds cleared again and the moon shone down, I found myself staring into a pair of blazing yellow eyes.

Trembling, I backed slowly away. As I did so, the snarling grew louder and the dark silhou-ette rose against the skyline and tensed.

It – whatever it might be – was getting ready to pounce . . .

CHAPTER 4

$\mathcal{U}$p in the sky, the scudding clouds swept across the great silver orb of the full moon, sending its rays fanning out across the rooftops. And in the crisp, silver light I saw the glint of dripping fangs and polished claws. I drew the sword from my ebony cane, my mind racing.

Whatever it was staring back at me from the roof-ridge opposite was huge, malevolent, and clearly out for blood. As I levelled the point of my blade between those two blazing eyes, my mouth drier than a stonemason's bench and my heart hammering like a bailiff's fist, I was never-theless intrigued.

As a tick-tock lad and a seasoned high-stacker, I was no stranger to the savage feral creatures that haunted the darker recesses of the city. I'd fought rats the size of tomcats, been attacked by sea eagles in the Eastern Quay, and even trapped a pair of blue-faced baboons that had escaped from J. W. Pettifogg's Exhibition of Wild Beasts.

But this creature was different. There was something unnatural about its huge size and hideous stare. Something unspeakably evil . . .

And then it pounced.

One moment I was standing there, sword raised, knees trembling. The next, in a blur of fur and fury, the hellish creature was flying towards me, its huge front paws extended and savage claws aiming straight at my hammering heart.

All I could say with certainty in those

The creature was silhouetted against the full moon…

heart-thumping seconds was that it was large – far larger than I'd expected. With its long legs, massive head and monstrous barrel-chest, it was clear that this was no ordinary animal.

At the last possible moment I stepped sharply to the left and jumped down off the parapet onto the flat roof below. Above me, I heard a clatter of claws and an angry snarl as the creature landed on the very spot where I'd been standing a moment before.

I turned and found myself staring once more into those fiendish yellow eyes. The creature was silhouetted against the full moon, a menacing black shape moving towards me.

I backed away, my sword still held out before me. The black shape came closer. Across the roof we moved – me backing up, the creature advancing – as the moon came and went with the passing of the scudding clouds . . .

All at once I was aware of a searing pain at the top of my right arm – my sword arm – of such intensity that I couldn't help but cry out. I glanced round to see that I had reversed into a metal chimney. It was so hot that it had burned through the material of my jacket and branded my skin. The sweet, pungent odour of my own burning flesh filled my nostrils, making my head swim and my legs go weak – but I knew that if I fainted, I'd be lost.

I stepped carefully round the smoking chimney and glimpsed a skylight glowing in the rooftop just beyond. It was my only hope.

I inched my way back towards it, slashing and stabbing at the shadowy creature all the while, keeping those great slavering jaws at bay. Then, as my heels reached the edge of the skylight, I paused for an instant and lowered my sword.

Just as I hoped, my monstrous pursuer

took the bait. With a hideous snarl, it pounced once more – only for yours truly to step aside like a matador dodging a charging bull. The great black shape flashed past me and hit the glass of the skylight, which shattered into a thousand jagged pieces beneath its weight. Moments later, there came a loud gloopy *splat!* from the chamber below.

I leaned forward and, taking care not to slip, looked down. Beneath me, a vast cauldron of glue was boiling, twists of steam dancing over the viscous brown liquid as it splattered and plopped. The next instant, a great glue-coated head broke the surface, its jaws open, emitting an agonized, blood-curdling scream before disappearing back into the depths of the cauldron.

At first I just knelt there, frozen to the spot, trying to clear my head and collect my thoughts. Not easy, I can tell you, what with the pain in my shoulder and the overpowering stench of the glue. It was only when the glue-sloppers and vat-paddlers on the factory floor below started shouting up at me that I was brought back to my senses.

'Oi, you up there!'

'What's going on?'

'What do you think you're doing?'

It was no time for explanations. Pulling back from the broken skylight, I retrieved my ebony cane, returned my sword to its sheath and beat a hasty – if shaky – retreat. The sound of angry voices soon faded as I continued to the edge of the factory roof and took a flying leap across the yawning gap beneath me, over to the jutting colonnade of the neighbouring building. Less than ten minutes later, I arrived on the roof of the tall gothic building that housed the chambers of Bradstock and Clink.

To my right was a tall thin drainpipe with a cough-candy twist that ran from the roof down to the pavement below. Normally I'd have grasped it and slid quickly down. But not that night. The pain at the top of my arm had become intense. It throbbed fearfully, and each time I moved my arm, the pain grew worse.

I had no option but to pick the lock of the door that led from the roof to the stairwell and take the stairs – and even that proved difficult. A task that would normally have taken me under a minute took me the best part of five. Eventually, though, the telltale *click* came, and I entered the stairwell of the tall building.

The offices of Bradstock and Clink were situated on the third floor. As I emerged from the staircase, the door – with the lawyers' two names etched in gold lettering on the glass panel, one beside the other – was before me. I collected myself as best I could, knocked and entered.

Young Mr Bradley Bradstock and old Mr Aloysius Clink were sitting in their usual places, at desks set against the wall on either side of a small grimy window. They both looked up.

'Ah, Barnaby,' said old Aloysius Clink, leaning back in his chair. He pulled his fob-watch from the pocket of his threadbare waistcoat and examined it ostentatiously. 'Come for your wages, eh?'

'Yes, sir,' I replied. 'All the summonses have been delivered and signed for.'

Young Bradley Bradstock had climbed to his feet, picked up a sealed envelope from the top of the filing cabinet behind him and was crossing the room in my direction. With the envelope containing my wages in one hand, he extended the other hand towards me – only to recoil in horror.

'My dear fellow!' he exclaimed. 'What in the name of all that is sacred have you done to yourself?'

'Oh, this,' I said, trying to sound dismissive. Certainly I had no intention of telling the two gentlemen about my encounter with the wolf creature. 'Bit of an accident. I ran into the glue works chimney. It's nothing, though. Just a little burn . . .'

But Bradley Bradstock wasn't going to take no for an answer. He handed me my wages and then turned his attention to the burn beneath the ripped and scorched material of my jacket.

'But this is awful,' he said. 'Take a look, Mr Clink.'

His business partner was beside him a moment later, tutting sympathetically.

'It does look nasty, Mr Bradstock,' he murmured, shaking his head.

'You'll need to see a doctor,' said Bradley Bradstock. 'Get something for it . . .'

'And in the meantime, Mr Bradstock, perhaps young Barnaby here would benefit from a spoonful of my own curative cordial.'

Mr Clink strode back to his desk and

pulled out a small blue bottle with a glass stopper and a black and silver label that I recognized at once.

'Doctor Cadwallader's Cordial,' Mr Clink beamed, preparing to pour me a spoonful. 'It's done wonders for me, dear boy. Haven't felt so good in years.'

I held up a hand to stop him. 'Thank you, Mr Clink' – I smiled weakly – 'but I haven't been a clerk errant all these years without picking up my fair share of cuts and scrapes. I'll take care of this myself, if it's all the same to you.'

'Whatever you say, Barnaby. Whatever you say. But you could do worse than consult the good Doctor Cadwallader in person – and have him send me the bill.' Mr Clink smiled. 'You're a fine tick-tock lad and I wouldn't want to lose you!'

He handed me a small gilt-edged card. At the top left-hand corner was a small disc, like the sun, with rays fanning out across the rest of the card. I read the words, written out in neat black italics:

Dr Theopholus Cadwallader
27 Hartley Square

I thanked him kindly and, with the envelope containing my day's wages tucked away in an inside pocket of my coat, I bade farewell to Messrs Bradstock and Clink and set off for my rooms.

While I had no intention of visiting some high-priced quack, I was touched by the old gentleman's concern for my health. All I needed, though, was a cold compress and a good night's sleep.

My injured arm made it too risky to attempt highstacking across the rooftops – particularly as a soft drizzle was starting up again, making the stacks and tiles slippery.

And so it was that I took the more conventional route home along the streets, heading up from the south-west quarter to my attic rooms in the north of the city.

As fate would have it, I found myself passing the corner of Water Lane and Black Dog Alley, which is where I saw it, outside the wedge-shaped building on the corner. It was scratched and battered, with one leg splintered and the arms and back splattered in blood – but it was unmistakable.

I stopped in my tracks. My jaw dropped and my heart started thumping furiously in my chest. For there on its side, abandoned in the gutter, was Old Benjamin's chair.

CHAPTER 5

$\mathcal{I}$ crouched down and inspected the over-turned coachman's chair more closely. It's amazing the wealth of information that can be gathered from seemingly innocuous objects if they are examined carefully enough.

The worn groove on the casing of a pocket watch, the soot on a footman's glove and a trailing thread on the hem of an elegant gown can all speak volumes to a careful observer. They can tell, for example, of a mine-owner's beautiful daughter stepping from a carriage held open by a footman with a jagged thumbnail; of tragic love, of bitter betrayal and the bloody consequences that almost broke a certain tick-tock lad's heart . . .

Like I said, it's amazing what objects can tell you, if you examine them carefully enough.

Looking over Old Benjamin's chair, I found deep gouges in the smooth wood at the armrests. The long curling splinters suggested they had been made by a sharp, curved instrument. A carpenter's knife, perhaps. A jemmy or a bradawl. Or perhaps, I thought as I saw where the gouges were parallel to one another, a pronged tool, like some kind of rake?

Or – my heart started thumping all over again – might they have been made by claws?

The left leg was broken. Probably, I thought, as a result of the chair being toppled into the gutter with some force. Droplets of blood had soaked into the upholstery and stained the material from the armrests to the high back of the chair. And stuck to it in numerous places were thick black hairs. Several of these I carefully removed, folded up in a piece of scrap paper and placed in the breast pocket of my poacher's waistcoat.

I stood up and tutted softly. A picture was beginning to form in my mind: a picture of Old Benjamin dozing in his coachman's chair beneath a silvery full moon . . .

Suddenly a huge creature with blazing yellow eyes and a thirst for blood bounds round the corner. Before Old Benjamin knows what's hit him, the creature is upon him, clawing and biting. The coachman's chair crashes into the gutter . . . The hellhound dashes off . . . Through an open doorway it runs, into a stairwell and up onto the rooftops to howl at the moon – which is where I encountered it. Meanwhile outside his building – a stone's throw from the glue factory – Old Benjamin, shocked and bleeding, crawls off to get help . . .

There are a thousand and one ways to meet your end in this city. According to statistics I've read, drinking unclean water or falling asleep beside a faulty gaslight are the most common, if least dramatic, ways. I've certainly seen a few grisly deaths in my time, I can tell you. Everything from out-of-control mill engines to the bloody flux. But being ripped apart by a savage beast would certainly count as one of the more unpleasant ways of departing this earth.

There was only one problem with my theory. If Old Benjamin *had* been ripped apart, there would have been far more than the few spatters on the chair, and surely a trail of blood leading away from it. But though I examined the surrounding pavement closely, I could see nothing. Not a trace. Old Benjamin, it seemed, had simply vanished.

'Vanished!' came a screechy, coarse-sounding voice, as if echoing my thoughts.

I turned to see Old Benjamin's ratty landlady, Mrs Endicott, standing in the doorway of her building, her arms folded belligerently.

'In the middle of the night!' she ranted. 'Done a moonlight flit without so much as a by-your-leave!'

She was a thin, shabbily dressed woman in a filthy cap that did not quite restrain her red tangle of dyed hair. A clay pipe protruded from her toothless mouth and wobbled above a bewhiskered chin as she talked.

'Was Old Benjamin behind on his rent?' I asked.

Mrs Endicott took a suck on her pipe. 'Not any more than usual,' she said. 'But I knew something was up. He'd changed these last weeks. A new man, he was! Full of vim and vigour, just like someone half his age! Perhaps he went off in search of adventure.' She sniffed. 'Could have said something first, mind ...'

'When did you last see him?' I asked, making a mental note to check out whether anyone had been admitted to the City Paupers' Hospital or the Benevolent Hospice for Retired Coachmen at the back of Inkhorn Court.

Mrs Endicott scratched her hairy chin thoughtfully. 'About an hour ago, ducks.' She gave me a gummy smile, then her look became quizzical. 'He was out here, sitting on this chair of his, gazing up at the moon and chuckling away to himself when I looked out of my window. I went to bed, and the next thing I know, I'm being woken up by a fearful howling and a loud crash.'

'Howling and a crash,' I repeated thoughtfully.

'But when I looks out, the street's deserted,' Mrs Endicott continued. 'I thought nothing more about it until a little while ago. I couldn't sleep for fear that Old Benjamin had gone to bed with the gaslight not turned off properly. I'm telling you, it wouldn't be the first time, neither. So I went down to his rooms and knocked, and, getting no reply, I went in, and Old Benjamin had . . . just . . . well, just sort of . . .'

'Vanished?' I suggested helpfully.

'Done a moonlight flit!' Mrs Endicott said firmly.

'Message for Mr Benjamin Barlow!' came an oafish voice just behind us.

We both turned.

There, ambling down the street as if he had all the time in the world, was an untidy, overweight tick-tock lad in an embroidered waistcoat and gleaming, wide-brimmed Kempton.

'Benjamin Barlow's not at home at present,' I said smoothly. 'But I'd be happy to pass the message on to him.'

The tick-tock lad yawned and scratched his head. 'It's all the same to me,' he said.

He casually plucked an envelope from the

hatband of his Kempton and handed it over with pudgy fingers, glistening with pie-grease.

I took the envelope with distaste between finger and thumb and looked at the bold, florid writing on the front.

Mr Benjamin Barlow
1 Black Dog Alley

URGENT

To be delivered by hand before lamplighting

'But this is *hours* late . . .' I began.

The oafish tick-tock lad just smiled and, yawning, turned on his heels. 'Like I said, it's all the same to me,' he laughed.

As I watched him waddle slowly down the street in his ridiculous waistcoat and expensive hat, I permitted myself a wry smile. With tick-tock lads like that, I thought, too lazy to climb a wall, let alone a high-stack, I'd always be in business.

'Should we open it?' Mrs Endicott whispered conspiratorially, her voice full of curiosity and more than a hint of greed.

Of course, as a tick-tock lad, I would never dream of opening any of the notes and messages entrusted to my care. But in this case . . . Well, I wasn't just a tick-tock lad, was I? Not with Old Benjamin. I was his friend – and I was worried about him.

I broke the seal at the back of the envelope and pulled out the letter. As I unfolded it, I frowned. It looked just like the visiting card old Aloysius Clink had given me: stiff vellum, the borders edged with gold. At the top left-hand side was a sun-like disc, its rays fanning out across the paper, while at the top right was the name and address of the sender.

I fancy I must have stood there for some while, staring nonplussed at the familiar words. Then I heard Mrs Endicott's voice breaking into my thoughts.

'Read it out to me, there's a dear,' she was saying. 'My eyes ain't what they used to be . . .'

I nodded and cleared my throat.

'Dear Mr Barlow,

Please present yourself at my consulting rooms this evening no later than sunset for the completion of the treatment that, I'm sure you'll agree, has proved so efficacious.

I shall administer the final dose of my cordial by means of a syringe directly into the artery.

BE WARNED!'

These words were larger than the preceding ones, and underscored . . .

'Failure to receive this final dose could result

in side effects of the most unfortunate kind.
DO NOT BE LATE!
Yours sincerely . . .'

The letter was signed by the good doctor with a swirling flourish.

Theopholus Cadwallader
MD, MRs, RTL, FRCP

'Pity,' said Mrs Endicott, tapping out her pipe on the door frame and returning inside. 'I was hoping for a banknote or two. Still, good riddance! That's what I say.'

The door slammed shut.

I folded the letter and placed it in the hip pocket of my waistcoat. My shoulder was hurting badly and I was tired fit to drop. All I wanted was a peaceful night's sleep. But one thing I knew for certain: the next day I was going to pay the good doctor a visit.

*   *   *

When the shafts of sunlight broke through the crack in the curtains the next morning, I discovered that, despite the cold compress, my arm was still painful. Having climbed from my bed, I changed the dressing and strapped the whole lot up with lint and a bandage. It was not ideal, but so long as I didn't do anything too strenuous, I knew that it would hold up.

I dressed, crossed the room and threw open the windows, only to pause with a shudder. It was not, however, my shoulder that caused my momentary anxiety. No, that was going to be fine. It was the sight of the rooftop chimney stacks stretching away into the distance that made me tremble with foreboding as they brought back to me the full horror of the previous night.

Was what had happened to Old Benjamin connected to the note from Dr Cadwallader? I wondered. And if so, how?

There was only one way to find out. Picking up my swordstick and coalstack hat, I climbed out of the window and up onto the roof-ridge of my building. I glanced around, checking that the coast was clear, then darted off over the rooftop of the adjacent building.

Hartley Square was situated to the west, as were all the most opulent residences of the city. It meant that, since the prevailing winds came from the west for most of the year, the area remained free from the gut-churning stench belching from the breweries, glue factories, tanning yards, coal furnaces and gasworks that pockmarked the areas to the east. Orientating myself by the black, white and yellow city flag which fluttered at the top of the gothic Museum of Antiques, I headed off, highstacking across the rooftops, revelling in the sense of freedom as I jumped from building to building.

At a disused mission hall I scurried nimbly up a slate roof until I got to the ridge tiles at the top where, arms out at my side for balance, I sped along them – one foot directly in front of the other, taking care not to dislodge any mortar as I passed. I skirted a tall chimney stack, then skittered down the sloping edge to an ornate gutter. I leaped off the side of the roof of a tenement building, across an alley far below me, and onto the parapet of neighbouring office chambers, where I rolled over once, twice, before jumping back to my feet.

Nothing, but nothing, can compare with the exhilaration of highstacking across the teeming city on a brightly sunlit morning.

Older and grander than the tenements, the office chambers I had reached were decorated with rounded arches, turret-like pinnacles and jutting windows set into the pitched roof. I had crossed it and others like it many times before, and as I passed the windows, I glanced down at the rows of clerks and scriveners, thanking my lucky stars that I wasn't one of them, scratching my life away with a goose quill in one hand, an inkpot by the other and a piece of yellowed parchment inches before my nose.

By leaping from window gable to window gable, I soon reached the end of that building, where, for the first time, I hesitated. My normal route, I discovered, had been ruined by the sudden demolition of the surrounding tenements. It meant a detour.

As a tick-tock lad, you get used to the ever-changing patterns of the city. Neighbourhoods rise up, decay, turn to slums and are cleared – sometimes, it seems, almost overnight – only to be replaced by new buildings, rising even higher in their place. It's what makes the highstacks so exciting – if, at times, dangerously unpredictable. As a rule, though, I didn't highstack over buildings which were in the process of construction. I was experienced enough to know that that was asking for trouble. But once the rooftops were completed, they were all mine.

After all, as I said, there were very few of us highstackers left. There's Black-Eyed John to the east, and Toby Martin in the dockside area – though, to be honest, I hadn't seen him for at least a year and there were rumours going round that he'd retired. Most tick-tock lads were like the specimen I'd met the night before. Good-for-nothing cobble-stone-creepers!

Glancing around, I saw I didn't have to go far out of my way. A short dash, a small jump from a crumbling brick warehouse to a nondescript municipal building with lead guttering and a weather vane designed like a ship; a gilded campanile and a flying leap to the stepped parapet of a weigh station, and I was back on track.

Three large buildings and a row of shops later, I was almost at my destination. I knew I must be getting close. Even up here in the rooftops, it was clear that the buildings were both better built and far more ornately decorated. As ever, pigeons and sparrows were my constant companions as I high-stacked it over this salubrious part of the city, flapping and squawking, indignant that a wingless creature should be invading their territory.

I performed what we highstackers call a Rolling Derby – a half-somersault followed by a one-legged standing pivot at the top of a vertical stanchion. It was a tricky manoeuvre but one that, once mastered, opened up even the highest rooftops as possible routes. Then, with a forward thrust of my arms, I took a flying leap off the edge of the pitched roof . . .

When I landed a moment later, I felt a sharp twinge at the top of my arm and winced with pain. I was above Hartley Square. I shinned down a series of drainpipes and pillars, before landing lightly on the

I performed what we highstackers call a Rolling Derby.

pavement directly in front of the black railings of number 27.

Elegant, dangerous and very, *very* quick – I tell you, highstacking is the only way to travel!

I was so pleased with myself as I stood there, dusting myself off, that I felt like taking a bow – even though there was no one around to appreciate my skills. At least, that was what I thought . . .

''Allo, 'allo, 'allo,' came a sarcastic-sounding voice, deep and rough. 'Where did you spring from, eh? I hope sir hasn't been . . .' his top lip curled, '*highstacking.*'

It was one of the local policemen, as ornate and polished in his top hat and brass-buttoned topcoat as the neighbourhood he patrolled. Here in the poshest part of town they got touchy about a tick-tock lad tramping over their rooftops. The policeman glared at me accusingly.

'No, no,' I said, trying not to sound out of

breath and hoping that he wouldn't notice the telltale brick dust on my elbows and knees. 'Only a fool would take to the rooftops rather than avail himself of our city's excellent coach-and-four omnibuses.'

The policeman frowned. 'Yes, well, perhaps sir would like to accompany me to the station, where he can give a statement to that effect, as well as explaining the exact nature of his business in Hartley Square.'

'I'm afraid I don't have time, Constable,' I said, with as much authority as I could muster. 'You see, I have an appointment with Doctor Cadwallader . . .' I pulled the card old Mr Clink had given me out of the breast pocket of my waistcoat.

'And what would a highstacking tearaway such as yourself want with an eminent Hartley Square physician?' The policeman leered at me nastily.

'Don't you think that is *my* business, Constable?' came a second voice.

The pair of us turned to see a tall, elderly gentleman descending the marble staircase of number 27. He had long white hair, parted in the centre, a pale, almost chalky pallor to his face and a pair of tinted pince-nez spectacles.

'Can't be too careful these days, sir,' the policeman said, twirling his black moustache authoritatively.

'Indeed, Constable,' said the gentleman. 'But the lad has told you he has business with me.'

'That's all well and good, Doctor,' the policeman blustered, rapidly reddening in the face. 'But he's been highstacking – I can tell. Look at the brick dust, sir, on his elbows and knees . . .'

'That is no concern of mine. What *is* of concern to me,' said the doctor, removing the pince-nez from his long thin nose and fixing the policeman with his piercing grey eyes, 'is what the chief constable's reaction will be when he hears that one of his men has been hampering my medical duties. Did I mention what a very good friend I am of the chief constable . . . ?'

The policeman visibly shrank. 'All right,' he said. 'Just this once I'll turn a blind eye.' He glared at me, his eyebrows knitted together. 'But let me catch you up on them rooftops again and I'll throw the book at you, my lad. Understand?'

I smiled and nodded. Muttering under his breath, the policeman turned away.

'Come,' said Dr Cadwallader, taking me by the arm with a surprisingly firm grip and leading me up the marble steps to his front door. 'Now tell me, what is so pressing that you had to climb over the rooftops to consult me?'

CHAPTER 6

*D*r Cadwallader locked the front door behind him and led me across the hallway to the sweeping flight of stairs. It was a magnificent place all right, with a black and white marble floor and a crystal chandelier overhead. And as for the staircase, its sumptuous carpet and ornate gold banisters wouldn't have looked out of place in a palace.

As we climbed the stairs, I noticed the expensive brass plaques on each of the landings. DR THADDEUS GRACE — EAR, NOSE, THROAT AND SPLEEN SPECIALIST; DR FENG-LI — HERBALIST AND ACUPUNCTURIST; DR MAGDI-KHAN; DR

SIBELIUS; DR P. J. DOOLEY; DR ASTLEY-SPUME —
each one with some impressive-sounding
speciality to do with ailments and parts of
the body I didn't even know existed:
CIRCULATORY AND PULMONARY MYOPATHIES;
SPECIALIST IN DISEASES AND DISORDERS OF THE
SUB-ILIAL TRACT; HAEMATOMAS AND SUB-
CUTICLE OEDEMAS . . .

Dr Cadwallader caught me looking at that
last one and gave a wry chuckle. 'Impressed?'
he said.

I nodded.

'Yes, Doctor Astley-Spume is in fact a
leading specialist in . . . pimples!' He smiled.
'The young ladies adore him.'

He strode on up the stairs with surprising
agility for a man of his age. I trotted behind.

Dr Cadwallader's chambers, I discovered,
were right at the very top of the building
and, fit as I was, what with the long journey
over the rooftops I'd just undertaken, I
have to admit I was getting slightly out of

breath. Dr Cadwallader, on the other hand, was as cool and collected as a fishmonger's cat.

'Here we are,' he said smoothly, removing a brass key from the pocket of his waistcoat and inserting it in the lock.

I glanced at the plaque beside the door. It was smaller than the one it had replaced and there was a thin strip of old floral wallpaper remaining from a previous period of decoration framing the brass nameplate – a sure sign that it had only recently been screwed into place.

DR THEOPHOLUS CADWALLADER, it announced. PHYSICIAN.

I liked its simple modesty. Once again Dr Cadwallader caught my glance.

'I have no need of florid titles, young man,' he said, a trace of a smile playing on his lips. 'I prefer my work to speak for itself.'

The doctor turned the handle and pushed the door open. As I was ushered inside, I was struck by the smell of fresh paint.

'How long have you had consulting rooms here in Hartley Square?' I asked.

'Not long,' he said, the hint of an accent in his rich, throaty voice. 'I have travelled widely in the East, and practised the healing arts in towns and cities, both large and small . . .' Dr Cadwallader paused and then gave a dry little laugh. 'But here, my dear young fellow, in this great, bustling city of yours, there are so many more opportunities for a simple physician such as myself.'

He motioned for me to follow him.

The shadowy, somewhat austere corridor led into a large chamber that I took to be a waiting room. There were six rather shabby red chairs with frayed gold piping and tassels standing with their backs to the wall, and one low table in the centre of the room, a selection of worn and faded periodicals upon it. I glanced at the titles. The *Hightown*

Intriguer, the *Weekly Journal for Ladies of Quality* and *The Swell* – high-class fashion rags and scandal sheets the lot of them, though judging by the dust that covered their yellowing pages, they hadn't been read in quite some time. Despite the swanky address, business appeared slow for the good doctor.

On the far side of the room was a second door, which opened to reveal Dr Cadwallader's study.

'Come on through,' he said amiably. 'And you can tell me the nature of your business with me, Mr . . .'

'Barnaby, sir. Barnaby Grimes.'

'Mr Barnaby Grimes, eh?' he repeated. 'Well, take a seat, Mr Grimes, and then let's have a little chat about the nature of your ailment.'

I did as I was told, sitting down on the upholstered leather chair in front of the desk.

Now, I've seen the inside of a few quacks' studies in my time – running errands and delivering prescriptions – and to be honest, this one was pretty typical of its kind. There was a tall brass oil reading lamp on the desk to the left of the blotter; two framed certificates hung on the wall behind it. To my right stood a padded examination table, a large print above it depicting the rudiments of a human body – bones to the left, muscles to the right.

It was the dresser on the far wall that had me smiling, though. Tall and imposing, its shelves lined with glass pots, bottles and stoppered vials of various shapes, sizes and colours, differing amounts of liquid in each one, it was the essential prop for every sham apothecary and fake doctor in the city.

Dr Cadwallader, meanwhile, had sat down on the high-backed leather chair behind the desk and turned up the desk lamp, enveloping the pair of us in a dim yellow glow.

'That's better,' he said with a smile. He leaned forward, elbows on the desk. 'Now, what can I do for you?'

'I don't have an ailment,' I said coolly, feeling those piercing grey eyes boring into mine from behind the tinted pince-nez. 'But I do have *this*.'

I retrieved the letter from my waistcoat pocket, unfolded it and passed it across the desk. Dr Cadwallader adjusted his pince-nez and began reading. I saw his brow furrow.

'Just how did you come by this?' he asked at length, his voice high-pitched and querulous as he peered at me over the top of his glasses.

'A great oaf of a tick-tock lad gave it to me outside Mr Benjamin Barlow's building last night—'

'Last night?' said Dr Cadwallader, his left eyebrow raised. 'And Mr Barlow?'

'Old Benjamin has vanished. I believe he was the victim of a vicious attack,' I said. 'As you are his doctor, I wondered whether he might have sought medical help from you?'

'Alas, no, Mr Grimes,' said Dr Cadwallader, shaking his head. 'What's more, when he failed to turn up for his final treatment, I struck him from my lists.' He stroked his chin thoughtfully. 'A vicious attack, you say?'

'There were signs of a struggle,' I said. 'Blood. Claw and tooth marks. An over-turned chair . . . And I happen to know that a wild animal was roaming the area that night, because I ran into it up on the rooftops of Greville's glue factory and killed it.'

'How fortunate!' exclaimed Dr Cadwallader, falling back in his chair.

'Fortunate?' I said.

'That such a vicious creature is dead,' said the doctor. He smiled smoothly, his thin lips pulled back tautly over his long, yellowed teeth. 'And tell me, how exactly *did* you manage to kill it?'

'It was chasing me over the rooftops,' I explained. 'I ducked and it crashed through a skylight into a glue vat.' I shrugged. 'Boiled down to the bone by now, I shouldn't wonder.'

'Excellent, excellent,' smiled Dr Cadwallader – then checked himself and, frowning, sat back. 'Of course, I'm devastated to hear of Mr Barlow's disappearance. As you can see from my letter, I do stress to my clients the importance of completing the treatment. Without the final injection to fix the invigorating effects of my cordial permanently, they quickly fade, leaving the patient in a state of advanced collapse . . .' He shook his head. 'If only that wretched clerk errant had delivered my summons to Mr Barlow in time, perhaps the poor man wouldn't have fallen prey to this rooftop creature of yours.'

'It wasn't *my* creature,' I said quietly. 'I only killed it.'

'Quite so,' said the doctor, with a thin grin. His brow furrowed thoughtfully. 'Up on the rooftops, you said. Do you make a habit of clambering over chimneypots, Mr Grimes?'

It was my turn to smile. 'Indeed I do,' I said. 'I'm a tick-tock lad – a clerk errant – and I like to take the shortest route from A to B.'

I could see by the doctor's expression that he was intrigued. The tick-tock lad he'd employed clearly wasn't up to the job, and now yours truly had come waltzing into his consulting rooms. I waited for him to take the bait. It didn't take long.

'Wait there, Mr Grimes!' said the doctor, climbing to his feet and disappearing through the door behind his desk, leaving it slightly ajar.

I peered after him into a darkened room. From what I could make out, it looked like

'This,' he said proudly, 'is my cordial.'

some kind of laboratory. A couple of moments later he was back, one of the silver-labelled blue bottles in his hand.

'This,' he said proudly, 'is my cordial. The result of many long years of research and experimentation.' He held the bottle up. '*An efficacious elixir for the enhancement of mental and physical powers,*' he said, reading the words off the label. 'It does exactly what it says on the bottle.'

I nodded. 'Old Benjamin certainly thought so,' I told him. 'I spoke to him only yesterday and he said he'd never felt better. And his cough had cleared up completely.'

'I'm pleased to hear it,' the doctor began. 'I'm only sorry he was unable to complete his treatment. Poor Mr Barlow. Remarkable head of hair for someone of his age . . .'

The doctor's cool grey eyes took on a faraway look for a moment before he continued.

'You see, Mr Grimes, unlike the high-priced quacks downstairs who peddle expensive potions to the rich, I reserve my cordial for those who need it most. The poorest and neediest in this great city; the ones who, if they disappeared off the face of the earth, would be least missed.'

He sat back in the chair and breathed deeply, his eyes closed.

'The ridiculous fake array of potions you see on the shelves behind me are for my rich clients – though, heaven knows, they're few and far between, what with the competition I face from downstairs. Times are hard and money is scarce, Mr Grimes.'

I put on an expression of polite interest and nodded.

Dr Cadwallader pushed the pince-nez up the bridge of his nose and fixed me with those steely grey eyes of his.

'If my work is to be successful, it is absolutely imperative that these consultation reminders reach my patients at the right time,' he told me. 'It strikes me that you might be just the lad for the job, Mr Grimes.'

'That struck me, too, Doctor.' I grinned. 'I'd be delighted to serve as your tick-tock lad.'

'Excellent, excellent,' said Dr Cadwallader, smiling broadly as he settled back in his chair. He pulled a small black notebook from his jacket pocket and a calendar from his drawer. 'Now let me see,' he said thought-fully, checking one against the other, and scribbling down notes with a small pencil. 'New course of treatment to start this Mon-day ... twenty-six days ... plus ... which would make it ...' He looked up. 'I would need you here three weeks on Tuesday, at seven o'clock in the morning.'

'I'll be here, sir,' I said. 'You can rely on me.'

The doctor nodded. 'I believe I can, Mr Grimes,' he said. He reached into an inside pocket and pulled out a wallet, from which he removed a blue and white banknote, unfolding it in front of my eyes. 'I trust this will be enough to retain your services, Mr Barnaby Grimes,' he said, a twinkle in his eye as he handed me the money across the desk.

'Yes, sir. Indeed, sir,' I said. 'Thank you, sir.'

'Oh, and, Mr Grimes,' he said, his voice hushed, yet insistent. 'I'm sure I don't have to tell you of the importance of discretion in this matter. The confidentiality of patients is, to every doctor, paramount, and mine more than most. So no loose talk, my lad, you understand me?'

'Of course, sir,' I said, sounding a little wounded.

Just then the bell above the entrance door began to tinkle. Moments later, in swept a small, elegant woman in a flowing satin dress and a short, expensive-looking jacket with

Westphalian trim, her golden hair piled high and held in place with several large tortoise-shell combs. Two young female attendants were in tow – the fairer of them, I noticed, particularly pretty . . .

'Madame Scutari!' Dr Cadwallader exclaimed, jumping up from behind the desk and marching towards her, coat-tails flapping and hand extended.

Rather reluctantly Madame Scutari held out her own hand, which the doctor took, raised to his lips and kissed chastely.

'Always an honour and a pleasure, my dear lady,' he announced, and I wondered whether this was one of the rich patients he fobbed off with sugar-water.

'Let's forget the formalities, Theo. I was passing in my carriage,' she said. 'Have you got anything for me?'

Her voice was imperious and shrill. Yet behind the cut-glass vowels I thought I detected a humbler background.

'Patience, my dear lady,' Dr Cadwallader said. 'The process cannot be hurried if one wants results.' He shot me a furtive look. 'Need I remind you how important discretion is in this matter?'

'Never mind that, Theo,' snapped the woman with a toss of her golden head. 'I've paid you handsomely on account, and I've got clients of my own who are getting impatient—'

'My dear Madame Scutari,' protested Dr Cadwallader, 'I'm working as fast as I can, I assure you.'

There was a low hiss as Madame Scutari breathed in sharply through her large white teeth. Dr Cadwallader shrugged apologetically.

Madame Scutari pulled herself up as tall as she could, tilting her head backwards as she did so, and flounced towards the door. 'I don't care how you do it,' she said, 'but I want what you promised me by the end of the week. Otherwise you'll have my cousin, the mayor, to deal with. Understand?'

With another toss of her head, Madame Scutari disappeared through the door, followed by her young ladies-in-waiting – but not before I caught the eye of the pretty one with the fair hair.

She smiled. I smiled back.

I turned to find Dr Cadwallader looming over me, his upper lip twitching and his steel-grey eyes lit up behind his pince-nez.

'You'd better go, Mr Grimes,' he rasped. 'I have work to do.'

CHAPTER 7

As I left Dr Cadwallader's dusty consulting rooms, I had plenty to think about. I had seen enough to tell me that something fishy was going on – something wet, scaly and stinking worse than workhouse fish-head stew. What was more, I intended to sniff it out. I had three weeks before the job for Dr Cadwallader, and a full roster book . . .

But first, there was Old Benjamin. I wasn't about to forget about him.

So I did as I'd promised, checking out both the City Paupers' Hospital and the Benevolent Hospice for Retired Coachmen – as well as the Wellesley

Infirmary for the Indigent for good measure.

All to no avail.

Wherever I went, the story was the same. No one had heard of anyone by the name of Benjamin Barlow. Like many others before him, the old-timer had, it seemed, simply disappeared without a trace.

And yet the strange events of that night kept gnawing away at me. What was left of that hellhound had probably glued a thousand labels onto a thousand ale bottles by now, but I couldn't get the image of its evil yellow eyes out of my mind.

Two weeks later I was still shivering at the thought as I sat at the feet of Sir Rigby Robeson—or rather, the statue of the pompous old rogue, which a grateful city had placed at the top of a tall column in Centennial Park. It was the perfect spot from which to count bullfinches for the eminent zoologist Professor Pinkerton-Barnes.

The professor – PB to his friends – was one of my more eccentric clients, though if truth be told, most of them were pretty odd. My first job for him had involved investigating the nests of magpies, and cataloguing the results. PB had some theory about the birds' predilection for silver teaspoons over other sparkly objects which, by my high-stacking skills and extensive notes, I was able to disprove. I had expected the professor to be disappointed, but far from it . . .

'Theories are there to be disproved, my dear Barnaby,' he'd said, smiling, combing his beard with thin, elegant fingers. 'How else are we to make scientific progress?'

Or recover Lady Phipp's stolen tiara? I thought. *And* pocket the reward? Another fascinating story I must get round to telling . . .

Anyway, this time the professor had a theory that the city bullfinches were growing unusually large and aggressive due to the recent introduction of the oriental tilberry tree – with its sweet and abundant fruit – into our parks and gardens. He believed that the cat population would soon be under threat. Well, several months spent observing and counting them from the top of Robeson's column had yielded plenty of information; unfortunately for PB, none of it relevant to the little stubby-beaked bullfinches with their elegant red breasts, grey shoulders and black and white wings.

I had observed that their favourite food was not the fruit of the towering oriental berry trees that surrounded the column, but rather the scraps they found when pecking about in fresh horse manure. As for drinking, it was the rainwater that collected in the brim of the hat at the top of the statue of Sir Rigby Robeson which they savoured above all other. And I carefully noted the size, habits and behaviour of four hundred and seventy-seven individual bullfinches . . .

Somewhat disappointingly, not one of these ever indulged in the aggressive behaviour the professor's theory alleged. Instead, it was the human inhabitants of Centennial Park who proved the more eye-catching. The shy meetings between chambermaids and footmen; the fine ladies parading the latest fashions – wide-brimmed bonnets and capes with Westphalian trim. And once, I remember, two rival governesses engaged in a ferocious duel with umbrellas . . .

It was when I was delivering my latest bull-finch observations – all twelve pages of them, neatly folded in the fifth pocket of my waistcoat – to the professor, that the mystery of Old Benjamin sprang into my mind. I reached into the second pocket and pulled out the small square of folded paper that contained the black hairs from the coachman's chair.

'Nesting material?' muttered PB as I unfolded the paper and laid the hairs carefully on the glass slide he had given me.

'Actually, no, Professor,' I said. 'This has nothing to do with your bullfinches. It's another case I'm working on.'

PB looked disappointed.

'I was wondering if you could identify the type of creature these hairs might have come from.'

'Pity,' he said. 'I was rather hoping a bull-finch had savaged a cat.' He shook his head. 'Still, leave it with me, Barnaby, and I'll see what I can do.'

I thanked him and climbed out of his laboratory window, then quickly shinned up the drainpipe. I was running late yet again. There was a week to go before my date with Dr Cadwallader and I hadn't had a minute to myself.

For the next five days I can honestly say I'd never been so busy. With bundles of summonses, writs, chits, wills, codicils and sworn affidavits tucked into my waistcoat pockets, and a list of addresses as long as your arm, I was highstacking throughout the city

'Pity,' he said. 'I was rather hoping a bullfinch had savaged a cat.'

with scarcely a moment to draw breath. There were jobs to be done for regulars I couldn't afford to let down, as well as some work for a couple of new clients who might, in time, prove to be nice little earners.

I remember there was a large collection of subscriptions I was organizing for Elijah Cope of *Cope's Practical Household Magazine* – very popular amongst the cooks and housekeepers of Hightown Square. And the more pressing matter of some book plates sent out by the Albion Publishing House, which had to be withdrawn after it was discovered that the engraver had depicted the Bishop of Gravetown answering the call of nature in the bottom right-hand corner.

As you can see, I was busy. Very busy. Yet not too busy to find a little time for my own research. Next to highstacking over the rooftops on a clear night beneath a full moon, there's nothing better than a few hours spent poring over dusty old volumes – and Underhill's

Library for Scholars of the Arcane had more than its fair share of books and dust.

Most of the library's subscribers were as dusty as the books themselves – half-mad alchemists, amateur magicians and ancient academics with an interest in phrenology or the properties of poison. Me, I go there to relax.

So there I was, in the basement of Underhill's Library for Scholars of the Arcane. Old Benjamin's disappearance and the yellow-eyed hound from hell were still playing on my mind, and I found myself being drawn to the familiar black leather-bound volumes of *Crockford's Journal of the Unnatural*.

Drawn from reports far and wide, *Crockford's Journal* was a quarterly review of strange sightings and unexplained incidents. I reached up and took down a volume. It contained bound editions of the journal from many years ago.

I flicked idly through the yellowing pages. All the usual stories were there – headless horsemen, cursed tombs and mysteriously abandoned lighthouses. Then, as I turned another page, I stopped. Something had caught my eye.

THE SINGULAR CAREER OF KLAUS JOHANNES WESTPHALE – WEREWOLF HUNTER

This journal regrets to report the death of the noted supernaturalist Dr Klaus Johannes Westphale, the werewolf hunter of Tannenburg. Justly famous for a long career pursuing that curse of the Eastern Forests, the lycanthrope, or werewolf, the good doctor was responsible for dispatching over three hundred of these accursed creatures and giving their human forms a decent burial.

Thanks to Dr Westphale, lycanthropy has become unheard of in recent times. Despite a small pension and income from articles and lectures, the doctor suffered hardship and poverty in his final years, before succumbing to his final illness – a wasting disease of the muscles that left him an invalid. Although he became increasingly bitter at his treatment by the authorities and people of Tannenburg, Dr Westphale's achievements remain unsurpassed.

This journal, for one, salutes a fearless soul and mourns his passing.

Beneath the short article was an engraving of a handsome-looking man with an intense gaze and black, flowing, shoulder-length hair.

The library was about to shut and the next day I had a seven-o'clock appointment with Dr Cadwallader. I scribbled a quick note of the volume and page number, and was just closing the book when I saw the date at the top of the dusty yellow page. This particular edition of *Crockford's Journal of the Unnatural* was ninety years old. Quietly I shut the book, replaced it on the shelf and left.

That following morning I was up bright and early. It was one of those breezy mornings when the weather – overcast one minute, sunny the next – didn't seem to know what it wanted to do. Thankfully, my shoulder was feeling much better. I changed the dressing again, just to be on the safe side, but it was clearly well on the way to healing.

I set off at six-thirty on the dot, arriving at 27 Hartley Square twenty-three minutes later.

Having highstacked over there, I toyed with the idea of entering the premises via the roof – but then thought better of it. Dr Cadwallader might consider it an intrusion. Instead, I entered in a more conventional fashion, having checked, this time, that there was no flat-footed constable to observe me descending the drainpipe.

'Ah, Mr Grimes,' Dr Cadwallader greeted me, his face breaking into a broad smile as he ushered me into his chambers. 'Right on time. Excellent! I've got the letters written out ready and waiting for you to deliver.'

He picked up an old battered medical bag that was lying on his desk, and pulled out half a dozen sealed envelopes, names and addresses written on them in a broad, florid script. He handed them over.

'Report back to me when you've delivered them all,' he told me.

'I shall, Doctor,' I said, and took my leave.

It was only when I was walking back down the great sweeping staircase that something about the doctor's battered old medical bag struck me. It was the initials, worn and faded, but still legible.

Three gold letters. N.J.W.

CHAPTER 8

So began one of the most fateful days of my career as a tick-tock lad; a day I still look back on with regret and shame. I was intent on uncovering the mystery of Old Benjamin's disappearance, yet still unaware of the terrible consequences of carrying out Dr Cadwallader's instructions.

If the doctor's surgery on Hartley Square was situated in one of the most salubrious quarters of the city, then a quick look at the addresses on the envelopes he'd given me was enough to confirm that my assignment would take me to some of the most squalid.

The good doctor's claim that he was helping the poorest and neediest people in the city seemed, on the face of it, to be true.

Just before Hartley Square hit the grand stretch of Duke's Avenue, I turned right down a narrow cobbled alley where I knew there was a drainpipe with particularly good handholds that would get me onto the rooftops in no time. Halfway up, I disturbed a big black tomcat, out on a window ledge, sunning itself. The creature hissed at me, its teeth bared and hair standing on end, furious that I had disturbed its peace and quiet.

I knew just how it felt. Whenever I was highstacking, I liked to imagine I was the only one up there, and that this rooftop world was mine and mine alone. Having reached the top gutter and climbed up onto the roof of the tall white building I had just scaled, I stood for a moment looking around. It was a beautiful, exhilarating sight all right, up here amongst the gables and spires. The

weather was warm, almost balmy, and overhead, plump puffs of cloud ambled across the
sky like stuffed ganders at a goose market.

'A perfect day for highstacking,' I muttered
to myself as, shielding my eyes with my
hand, I planned my route.

Far across the city I saw the place that I
was heading for. A brown blanket of sooty
filth hung over the whole area, with the
forest of great brick and metal chimneys
pumping out yet more smoke with every
passing second.

One city for the rich and one for the poor,
I thought.

I patted the envelopes in my inside pocket
and set off across the rooftops at a brisk pace.
Before long I was approaching my first drop.
Even if I'd had my eyes closed, I would have
known it. The air had the stale, pungent
odour of burning sea-coal, and a low, droning
underswell of human misery filled my ears.

I was drawing close to the Wasps' Nest.

One of the oldest parts of the city, the whole area had fallen into decay and disrepair. It was a hotchpotch of paper-thin buildings, crammed together so tightly that precious little sunlight penetrated the maze of stinking alleys below. Clapboard tenements rubbed shoulders with crumbling brick buildings, underground tunnels and attic rat runs linking one to the other to form a vast three-dimensional labyrinth through which its occupants buzzed and scurried.

And there were a lot of them. Tens of thousands, certainly – though no official city census had ever discovered just how many. In some of the dilapidated tenements whole families – grandparents and all – shared a single room. Buildings would collapse under the weight of the number of people who filled them, and there wasn't a single ledge, alcove, nook or cranny that wasn't put to use. In the Wasps' Nest, even the most wretched hole in the corner of the dingiest cellar would be furnished with a stool, bucket and straw mattress, and called 'home'.

Normally I had little reason to visit the Wasps' Nest. It was a dark, noisy, vicious place; swarming with thieves and cut-throats who, if provoked, were as bad-tempered as wasps themselves – but whose stings were far more deadly. Yet it was into this filthy, seething pit of humanity that I now descended, taking care to avoid the more hazardous crumbling ledges and rusting drainpipes that threatened to come away in my hand.

I made sure I kept my eyes peeled and my hand ready to unsheathe my swordstick at a moment's notice as I climbed down, leaving the sunny morning behind me and entering a shadowy, soot-filled gloom. And if it was gloomy outside, who knows what it must have been like inside those cramped build-ings all around me. After all, most of the windows were broken – some boarded up, some stuffed with rags – while those that miraculously were still in one piece were so thick with sooty grime that no one could see either in or out.

Nevertheless, what struck me most about the Wasps' Nest was the feeling of being watched. Sullen-looking men in battered stovepipes and tom-o'tassels, and half-starved waifs in ragged clothes watched from doorways and balconies through narrowed, suspicious eyes. I gripped my swordstick all the more tightly as I stepped down from a sooty ledge and out into a narrow alley.

A couple of street corners away was number 4 Seed Row, my first drop. It was, according to my list, where I would find one Edna Halliwell. As soon as I turned the second corner, I knew I'd found the right street. At one end of Seed Row there was a back yard where poultry was fattened – and it was that curiously stuffy odour of damp feathers which now filled my nostrils. As I got closer, the strangled-sounding clucking of the birds grew louder.

I was on Seed Row all right. I counted my way along the terrace and knocked on the fourth door. It remained shut – though I could hear the sound of movement coming from inside, like rats scurrying about under the floorboards. I knocked again, louder. This time the door flew open and I was confronted by a great ogre of a man with a stained vest and an eye-patch. A scrawny girl, clinging to his left leg, peered up at me.

'What you want?' the man grunted suspiciously.

'I have a letter for Edna Halliwell,' I told him.

'I'll take it,' the man said, thrusting out a filthy hand that looked as if it strangled geese for a living.

'Sorry, guv'nor.' I smiled. 'Has to be delivered by hand to Mrs Halliwell in person.'

'Mighty full of yourself for a tick-tock lad,' sneered the great oaf before his one good eye spotted my swordstick.

I let him check out the brass-tipped handle and the inch of gleaming steel blade that I had just exposed with a casual flick of my wrist. I smiled back at him and waited. The oaf blinked, then turned aside.

'Top of the house,' he growled. 'Knock loudly. Old Ma Halliwell's a bit deaf.'

I thanked him and stepped inside.

The stairs were rickety, and as I made my way up, I could feel them shift under my weight. It felt as though, like a house of cards, the whole lot might collapse at any moment. The building stank of boiled cabbage and burned fat – odours that seemed to get more intense as I climbed higher. I tried my best to ignore it – that and the eyes that peered at me through the banisters, out of the cracks in partially opened doors and from the shadows of every landing.

I knocked at the door at the very top of the building. It was opened instantly, and I was struck by a sour smell that left me gasping for breath.

'Yes?'

I found myself looking at a small, pale, ferret-faced woman. It was impossible to tell how old she was. Her hair, though unwashed, was thick and golden and could have belonged to someone young. Her skin, however, was ravaged – a leathery parchment of lines and pockmarks.

'Edna Halliwell?' I said, speaking loudly.

She nodded. 'Yes, yes, you don't need to shout. There's nothing wrong with my hearing – leastways, not any more . . .'

I reached into an inside pocket of my coat and handed her the letter. 'From Doctor Cadwallader,' I told her.

She nodded, and smiled delightedly. Using a dirty fingernail, she opened the letter and read it, her lips moving silently as she did so.

Glancing over her shoulder, I saw the cause of the overpowering smell.

The rafters of the attic room were crowded with nesting pigeons; hundreds of them, coming and going through holes in the roof as I watched. The floor and meagre furnishings were white with encrusted droppings, with more scraped into heaps or deposited in sacks in the corner. Old Ma Halliwell was obviously a ledge-scraper – earning her living by bagging and selling pigeon droppings for fertilizer.

'Tick me off your list, young man. I'll be there,' she said, breaking into my thoughts, and the door was pushed shut in my face.

One down, I thought as I put a tick next to her name.

I checked the next name and address. *Edward Dobbs. Basement, 12 Spieler Lane.* Returning the list to my inner pocket, I set off down the stairs.

Edward Dobbs, it turned out, was an old

barrow boy, down on his luck. When I say 'boy', old Edward must have been seventy if he was a day. He gave me a great gap-toothed smile when I presented him with Dr Cadwallader's reminder, and promised to present himself at Hartley Square that evening before the lamps were lit.

I left Spieler Lane and turned right. My third drop was beyond the Wasps' Nest, on Strap Street – above the Sow's Ear. A Miss Sarah Monahan, according to my list.

I climbed up a drainpipe onto the curving roofline of Amhurst Crescent and headed towards the gaslights of the theatre district. Before long I was approaching the smoking chimney stacks of Strap Street, with its crowded music halls, taverns and gambling dens. The Ambassador, Henry Moonshine's and the Bloody Nose and Bootleg were all to be found on Strap Street, along with dozens of other establishments just like them.

They all echoed with the sound of cursing and swearing, raucous laughter and bawdy song, and the banging and crashing of innumerable fist fights and bar brawls. Strap Street – even on a sunny day – wasn't for the faint-hearted.

I shinned down a copper pipe and jumped lightly from the water butt below, landing in a back alley just up the street from the Sow's Ear – a fitting name for a place from which no good would ever come. With its broken windows and rusting sign, I knew I was looking at an inn that had seen more than its fair share of trouble, and as I heard the raised voices and muffled thuds from inside, I prepared myself for flying fists and barstools.

Seizing the door handle with one hand and my swordstick with the other, I marched in.

I'm not sure what I was expecting. Perhaps that there would be a sudden silence and everyone present would turn and look at me.

Perhaps that someone would reel round from the bar and smash me across the head with a bottle the moment I crossed the threshold. Thankfully, nothing of the sort took place – in fact, I rather doubt anyone even noticed me, although since it was so dark, I couldn't say for sure.

I paused for a moment to let my eyes grow accustomed to the gloom, then crossed to the bar, where a swarthy woman with tattooed forearms the size of hams was busy drying tankards with a filthy rag. There was sawdust on the floor and smoke in the air. I sat myself down on a tall stool and rested my elbows on the battered oak counter.

'I have a letter for Sarah Monahan,' I said. 'I understand she has a room above this tavern.'

'Sarah Monahan?' the landlady repeated and shook her head, her filthy mobcap threatening to fall off into the tray of slops. 'No one of that name round here.'

I frowned. 'Are you sure?'

The woman glared at me furiously. 'Are you calling me a liar?'

Now the tavern fell silent and everyone turned and stared at me. Then I heard the sound of scraping chairs as three or four hefty-looking men climbed to their feet. One of them, I was sure, was gripping the neck of a bottle with one hand and tapping it softly in the palm of the other. It was looking like trouble. In rough houses like the Sow's Ear it didn't take much to trigger a fight.

I smiled casually, and laid a large coin on the counter.

'I'd never dream of calling a carnival legend such as yourself a liar,' I said. 'And I'd be honoured if I could buy a drink for such a work of art.'

The landlady beamed me a delighted black-toothed smile and motioned for the tavern thugs to resume their seats.

'So you've heard of me?' she asked coyly.

'Henrietta the Amazon Queen? Of course!' I said.

I'd noticed the gothic lettering that spelled out the name on her forearm. Clearly it formed part of a larger tattoo which, from its elaborate design, obviously spread up her arm – and, most likely, over the rest of her body. It told me everything I needed to know. The landlady had been a 'Painted Lady' and toured on the carnival circuit. Probably scraped up enough to buy this rundown tavern – a place where the compliments were most likely as rare as unwatered ale.

So I laid them on thick, and she loved it. I told her how exquisite the tattoo of the mermaid on her lower arm was – even though, truth be told, she looked as if she needed a shave. Two drinks later, Henrietta was my best friend in the world.

'A pleasure to meet you, Mr Grimes, I'm sure,' she said with a girlish giggle. 'And if I hear anything about this Sarah Monahan woman, I'll let you know.'

It was lunch time and I was hungry, so I ordered some sausages and mash, took them to a table over by the door – just in case I needed to make a quick getaway – and sat myself down. The sausages were better than they looked and the mash didn't have as many lumps as it could have had, given the type of dive I found myself in. I was just mopping up the last drops of gravy with the remnants of my bread when I felt someone tugging my arm.

I hadn't noticed anyone there, and I spun round suspiciously, ready to draw my sword if it looked like trouble – only to find myself faced with a short, black-haired woman with thin lips, a bulbous nose, tiny eyes and angry skin, blistered and flaking and the colour of a strawberry.

She must have seen the look of shock in my eyes, for she recoiled and turned away.

From the bar came the cackling laughter of the landlady.

'Don't you worry about Scaldy Sal,' she said. 'She won't do you no harm. Just collecting your plate, if you've finished. Caught in a furnace blast a few years back, she was, poor thing. Been sickly ever since.'

I turned back to the woman. 'I'm so sorry,' I said.

She shrugged and took my plate. 'I heard you,' she said softly. 'Earlier. Looking for me.' Her voice dropped to a hushed whisper. 'Sarah Monahan.'

The penny dropped. Sarah. Sal . . .

How typical, I thought, that in this dark inn even someone who worked here was known only by a nickname rather than the name they were given at birth. It was the perfect place to remain anonymous. I made to pull the envelope from my inside pocket, but she stilled my arm.

'Not here,' she whispered. 'I'll see you outside.'

I nodded.

Minutes later I bade farewell to the landlady and left the inn. Two dogs ran past, almost tripping me up; a small black and white one chasing a large brown one that had a dead rat clamped between its jaws. Two children were playing some kind of pat-a-cake game on the wall opposite.

'You have something for me.'

I looked round to find Scaldy Sal standing beside me again. She was certainly a past master at creeping up on folk.

'This,' I said, pulling the envelope from my coat pocket.

'A letter,' she said, turning the envelope over in her hand.

'From Doctor Cadwallader,' I told her.

'Ah yes,' she said, 'the final consultation. I'll be there.' She smiled, her yellow, peg-like teeth gleaming. 'The doctor's been so very good to me . . .'

With that, she turned and slipped away as softly as she had appeared. I set off in the opposite direction, heading for the riverside – where the fourth person on my list lived.

Ginger Tom Carrick.

His address was the most curious of the lot. The *Susie Lee*, Wharf 12, East Bank. Strangest of all, *Susie Lee* was written upside down.

Not that that was what gave me pause for thought. No, it was the fact that this fourth drop was down in the notoriously dangerous East Bank – a place that made the Wasps' Nest seem like a flower-seller's boudoir. I know every bit of the city and I'm telling you, that particular stretch of river was the very last place you'd ever want to visit, even on the sunniest of afternoons – unless, like me, you had no choice.

When I reached the river, I saw that the

tide was out, for the water was low and the mud banks exposed. Scruffy gulls wheeled overhead, mewling and screeching as I made my way along the towpath, counting off the wharves as I went past dilapidated warehouses and rundown shipwrights.

To my left, out on the freshly exposed mud, were legions of wiry boys and girls – barefoot and dressed in rags – searching for anything that they might salvage from the river flowing past. Mudlarks, they were called.

I shivered involuntarily.

The name used to describe them might sound innocent enough, but I'd had dealings with their like before. Feral urchins – orphaned or abandoned by their parents – who banded together in packs. Roaming the desolate mudflats, jealously guarding their patch of territory, they would sift through the flotsam and jetsam, trying to eke out a meagre living. They might look like children, but woe betide anyone who underestimated them for a moment. It wasn't unknown for a whole tribe of them to descend on hapless dockers or drunken sailors, emptying their pockets and leaving them bruised and bleeding – or worse . . .

They even had their own language – a guttural slang, snatches of which I'd picked up over the years. I'd had to. But even so, I remained wary. The East Bank was a place where the lowest of the low washed up, condemned to scavenge in the mud by a callous city. The mudlarks were as savage and unpredictable as they were resourceful and cunning. They had to be, just to survive. I kept my eyes trained on the stooped figures, squelching through the mud. They were some way off to my left, but I drew my sword just in case.

'Oi, you there!'

The voice had come from the opposite direction, and I turned to see two figures emerging from a rundown sail yard.

I turned to see two figures emerging from a rundown sail yard.

Although they were older than the scavenging children, I saw at once from their dark, weathered complexions and intricate chin tattoos that they had once been mudlarks themselves. Their waterproof ankle-length oilskin slickers and battered nor'westers, coupled with foppish, if tatty, double-knotted cravats and embroidered waistcoats, singled them out as river-toughs – the young thugs that the more vicious mudlarks graduated into. Violent jacks of all trades, they dabbled in all sorts of dealings, from press-ganging to kidnapping, smuggling and extortion.

As they drew closer, I could see they had swordsticks of their own – one with a pewter hound's-head pommel; the other with a wooden handle shaped like a beak.

'Well, well, well,' said the stockier of the two, stopping on the path just before me. 'Look what we got 'ere, Ginger, me old cocklemonger.'

The red-headed one giggled half-wittedly. I didn't have time for this.

'Skingle me, if it ain't one of 'em tick-tock lads from the smoky.' The stocky lad grinned. 'Pockets bulging wiv notes 'n' dockets, 'n' all sorts of sparklers.'

Ginger stopped giggling just long enough to ask, 'Fink 'e's got summat for us, do you, Ned?'

'Let's ask 'im.' As Ned spoke – his voice soft yet menacing – the pair of them unsheathed their swords, which glinted in the low afternoon sun. 'Fancy turning out them pockets, tick-tocker?' he said.

I eyed them both coolly. I didn't want a fight, yet it was beginning to look as though I had no choice in the matter.

'No need for roustabouts, my dear ink-chins,' I said. 'Why don't you sheathe up your slicers, I'll sheathe up mine – and I'll be on my way.'

Ned chuckled humourlessly. ''Ear that,

Ginger? 'E don't want no roustabout.' His expression hardened. 'We'll see about that, milk-face.'

Suddenly, as one, the pair of them lunged towards me, the tips of their swords aimed at my chest. With a resounding *clash*, I parried away both swords, stepped sharply to one side and, while the pair of them were momentarily off balance, launched an attack of my own.

Ginger didn't see me coming – until it was too late. He cried out with pain as the tip of my sword sliced through the sleeve of his oilskin slicker and drew blood. Howling, he fell to the ground. Ned was going to be more of a problem. Not only had his tough life left him hard as horse-tacks, but somewhere along the line he'd learned how to handle a sword. Sure enough, a moment later he lunged again.

It was a fierce yet reckless blow. I parried it away easily enough, but the blow jarred through my arm, sending darts of pain through the half-healed burn. Seeing my wince of pain, Ned let out a triumphant howl and launched a brutal attack, raining down blow after blow. I suspected that this was how he usually won his sword fights, battering his opponents into submission.

It wouldn't work with me.

Three, four, five times I parried his swinging blows, prodding him back with thrusts of my own each time. I didn't want to hurt him – but then again, I needed to teach this East Bank bully a lesson. Behind me, I heard Ginger still squealing with pain. To hear his high-pitched shrieks, you'd have thought I'd sliced his arm clean off instead of merely pricking his skin. In front of me, Ned was just where I wanted him.

'Waah!' he cried out a moment later as his left foot stepped back to the very edge of the towpath.

For a moment his arms flailed wildly as he

tried to regain his balance. I stepped forward and, with the point of my sword, prodded him gently in that gaudy waistcoat of his. With an angry roar, he fell back off the jetty and landed with a loud *squelch*. I sheathed my sword and tipped my hat as I looked down at him lying spread-eagled in the mud.

'I'll be bidding you good day, me old cocklemonger,' I said.

As I set off, I saw Ned scrambling round desperately in the mud for his sword. Ginger – clutching his shoulder and still howling – jumped down to give him a hand.

'I'll get you, tick-tocker!' Ned shouted after me, and waved a muddy fist. 'Ned Silver don't forget, and that's a promise!'

Deciding to give that part of the towpath a wide berth on my return, I continued along the river in search of the address on my list. It was only a few minutes later that I found it. The moment I did so, the reason the name had been written upside down suddenly became clear. The address where Ginger Tom Carrick lived was an upturned boat.

Bowed and blistered, the hull was riddled with so many worms that the light shone through from the other side. A small window had been cut into the portside bow near the front – but it hadn't been glazed. Instead, an awning fashioned from a broken umbrella had been nailed into place to keep out the worst of the weather. The door – low and warped so badly it was standing proud of the frame – was at the stern.

I knocked.

There came the sound of clinking china, a scraping of wood on wood – and the door opened. A man stood there, ruddy-faced, blue-eyed and with the reddest ginger hair I had ever seen.

'This is for you,' I said, peering inside as I handed over the letter.

The man scanned the envelope. *'Ginger*

Tom Carrick,' he said. 'Aye, that's me. And you are?'

'Barnaby Grimes,' I told him, 'tick-tock lad. I'm on a job for Doctor Cadwallader.'

'Oh, Doctor Cadwallader, God love him!' Ginger Tom exclaimed. 'The man's a miracle worker, so he is. Taken away all my aches and pains ... Why, not a month since, I was confined to my bed most of the time, arthritis so bad I was scarce able to walk. And now look ...'

He threw his arms up into the air and did a passable jig as I watched, a grin on my face. Of course, it was little wonder that his joints were so bad, living in these conditions. What with the rotting straw and newspaper on the damp mud, the lack of heating and, from the looks of it, nothing to eat save what the river threw up, it was a wonder the poor fellow was alive at all.

'Thank you for this, Barnaby Grimes,' he said, retreating into the upturned *Susie Lee.*

'And be certain to assure the good doctor that I'll be there this evening for that final syringe.' He grinned happily. 'I can't wait to be completely cured!'

Dr Cadwallader was certainly popular with his patients, I thought as I stopped outside my next drop, a rundown rooming house near the tannery yards. Scobie Rathbone – a thin man with dark, haunted-looking eyes – opened the door and smiled delightedly as I handed him the letter. I got another glowing testimonial to the miraculous powers of Dr Cadwallader's cordial from the old smoke-shed stoker, who had previously suffered years of ill-health, like so many in his line of work.

A single man, out of work and down on his luck, he'd run into the doctor outside a wig-maker's shop. Poor Rathbone had been reduced to selling the hair on his head to pay rent on his shabby room. Just like Old Benjamin, it was Rathbone's cough that had alerted Dr Cadwallader to his plight, and the man was presented with a bottle of cordial on the spot.

Was there no end to the good doctor's altruism? I asked myself. One last injection and his patients' miraculous cures would be complete. They would go happily on their way, with only their heartfelt thanks as reward. It all sounded too good to be true.

I, for one, wasn't buying it.

I headed slowly back towards the city. It had been a long day. One final drop and my day's work would be complete. At the far side of a line of warehouses I jumped up onto a low wall and scaled the side of the chandlery building to the roof. I glanced at my watch. The lamps wouldn't be lit for another hour. I had until then to complete my drops. I took out the list . . .

Mr A. Klynkowiczski, 21 Beale Terrace, I read.

That was a little row of houses not a hundred yards from Edna Halliwell's attic dwelling place on Seed Row. If only I'd noticed, I could have delivered this letter just after hers. It was an error worthy of an apprentice clerk, I told myself as I hurried through the streets back the way I'd come, passing the places I had seen earlier.

As I re-entered the Wasps' Nest, something curious occurred to me. All these streets and houses, which had looked so terrible earlier, suddenly didn't seem quite so bad after all – not compared to the mudflats by the river or the bawdy taverns of Strap Street.

I passed number 4 Seed Row, and turned right and right again onto Beale Terrace, stopping in front of number 21 and looking up. The house was tall and thin and it seemed that, unlike its neighbours, the whole lot was owned by one family. I rang the bell and waited.

From inside came the sound of footsteps running lightly down the flights of stairs. It was followed by the echoing *thump-thump* of someone crossing the hall to the front door. A bolt slid back. A latch clicked. The door opened and a face looked out.

'You!' I cried out, my jaw dropping with surprise.

CHAPTER 9

loysius Clink was, I must confess, the last person on earth I had expected to see here in the Wasps' Nest.

'Barnaby!' exclaimed old Clink, evidently as surprised to see me as I was him. 'What brings you to this neck of the woods?'

'This,' I said, pulling the final envelope from my waistcoat and handing it over.

'Ah,' he said, a slightly sheepish smile tugging at the corners of his mouth. 'Klynkowiczski. Yes, that's me. Shortened my name to Clink in the office. My reminder for the final consultation at Doctor Cadwallader's surgery, eh?'

I nodded.

'I'm honoured to have it delivered by the best tick-tock lad in the city,' he chuckled. 'Tick me off your list. I'll be there presently – just as soon as I finish my tea.'

'I had no idea you lived in the Wasps' Nest, Mr Clink,' I replied.

The old man smiled. 'I might be a successful lawyer, but I never forgot my roots, Barnaby. I was born in this house,' he said. 'An only child. My father was an honest tailor, and worked himself into an early grave to make sure I got a good education. I stayed on to look after my dear mother at first, but when she passed away, I just didn't have the heart to leave – even though, by then, I was a successful lawyer. Perhaps I might have if I'd married . . .'

His expression took on a wistful, faraway look. Then, as if remembering I was there, he focused on my face, his watery eyes twinkling.

'But that wasn't to be. I was always sickly,'

he said. 'Coming down with one thing or another. But then I met Doctor Cadwallader, right here in the Wasps' Nest, and tried his cordial. And . . . Well, you know how miraculous it is!'

I nodded. The old lawyer had never looked so healthy, despite the worn and patched clothes that in his offices seemed an eccentricity, but in these surroundings looked perfectly in keeping. No wonder, I thought, that Dr Cadwallader had mistaken him for a pauper and presented him with a course of his precious cordial.

'Doctor Cadwallader . . .' I ventured, as casually as I could. 'Has he ever asked for payment for his cordial? Or a final fee perhaps when the treatment is completed?'

Mr Clink shook his head. 'No, never,' he replied with a beaming smile. 'Of course, I, like you, Barnaby, was suspicious at first, but the good doctor said that his only wish was to bring relief from suffering, and that his good deeds should remain secret, and as you see' – the old lawyer jigged about before me in delight – 'Doctor Cadwallader's cordial does exactly what it says on the bottle.'

I left Mr Clink waving to me from the doorstep of his rundown house and promising not to be late, set off for Dr Cadwallader's consulting rooms – and a handsome fee for my day's work.

Whatever the miraculous properties of the cordial, I was more convinced than ever that there was more to the doctor's do-gooding than met the eye. But at that moment all I had were questions – questions, and the increasingly rancid smell of fish-head stew in my nostrils!

A while later I presented myself at Hartley Square. As I handed Dr Cadwallader my list, I noticed that he seemed a little distracted. Eddie Dobbs, Scobie Rathbone, Ginger Tom Carrick and Edna Halliwell were already there, and he was ushering them through his office to a chamber beyond.

'This way, this way. The syringes are ready, but first' – he smiled at them – 'a nice cup of tea . . .'

He guided them through the door, pulled it to, then turned to me. From his manner, I got the distinct impression that he was eager to be rid of me.

'Ah, Mr Grimes,' he said. 'Excellent work. I shall be needing your services again next month.'

I nodded.

'So that's agreed.' He glanced at his pocket watch. 'Two more patients and I can get started . . . That will be all, Mr Grimes.' He flashed me a brittle smile as he handed over a crisp banknote, and gently pushed me out into the corridor. 'Goodnight, Mr Grimes. Goodnight.'

'Goodnight, Doctor,' I called back casually over my shoulder as I made plenty of noise stomping down the stairs.

Once outside, I made sure to slam the

heavy front door and headed down Hartley Square and into Broad Street, with its fashionable shops. There, I planned to find a convenient drainpipe and shin back onto the rooftops. I needed a concealed vantage point where I could observe the doctor's consulting rooms unseen.

I was just sizing up the possibility of a deserted side alley to my right when I was stopped dead in my tracks by a pair of beautiful dark eyes staring out at me from a shop window. They belonged to the pretty young assistant I'd seen with Madame Scutari in Dr Cadwallader's consulting rooms.

I glanced up at the shop sign as I crossed the street. MADAME SCUTARI, it announced. BESPOKE GARMENTS FOR PERSONS OF QUALITY.

Sure enough, the shop dummies in the window were dressed in clothes that only the wealthiest men and women in the city would be able to afford. Elegant suits. Dresses of satin and toile. Embroidered silk blouses.

And tailored overcoats, each one made of the finest cloth and finished off with exquisitely lustrous fur – the much-sought-after Westphalian trim.

The bell chimed as I entered the shop.

'You look familiar. Do I know you?' the pretty shop girl asked, her cheeks colouring charmingly as she emerged from the window display.

'Barnaby Grimes,' I said with a small bow. 'We haven't been formally introduced, but I do the occasional job for Doctor Cadwallader. I saw you in his consulting rooms.'

She seemed to flinch at the sound of the doctor's name and grew pale. But then, pulling herself together the next moment, she smiled sweetly.

'Ellen. Ellen Wicks,' she said.

'Very pleased to make your acquaintance, Miss Wicks,' I said formally, and offered her my hand. I looked around. There were more coats on display, all decorated at the cuffs and

'Ellen. Ellen Wicks,' she said.

collars with the gleaming Westphalian trim – the very height of fashion that season among 'persons of quality'. 'Nice,' I said. 'Very nice. Business must be good.'

'That depends on Doctor Cadwallader,' said Ellen, looking away.

Before I could ask her what she meant, Madame Scutari herself flounced into the shop, talking loudly to a well-known society dowager.

'Step this way, my dear Mrs Ducressy,' Madame Scutari said, her voice ingratiating yet shrill. 'I want to show you this jacket. Cut on the bias and edged with a very rare auburn Westphalian trim. Absolutely to die for—' She caught sight of the two of us, and paused.

'Miss Wicks?' Madame Scutari's lip curled in a dismissive sneer. 'Does this . . . this . . . *clerk* have business in our establishment?'

'Just passing,' I said. I smiled, tipping my coalstack hat to all three of them, and stepping outside into the street – but not before giving the pretty Ellen a wink that had her blushing all the more.

I crossed back to the other side of the street and approached the alley I'd spotted earlier. A stout iron drainpipe rose up to the rooftops, and I was about to scale it when a hand clasped my shoulder. Fearing the worst, I spun round, expecting to see the reddened face of a constable.

'Barnaby Grimes!' Professor Pinkerton-Barnes's friendly face greeted me. 'I thought it was you. Just the man I was looking for.'

'You were, PB?' I said. 'It's just that I'm in the middle of something right now—'

He smiled absentmindedly. 'Indeed, lad,' he said. 'I have a new assignment for you.'

'Can we discuss it later, PB?' I said. But the professor's hand remained firmly clamped on my shoulder.

'Won't take a moment, Barnaby,' he said good-naturedly. 'Let's walk a while.'

Before I knew it, we had turned the corner of Broad Street and were heading towards Cutler's Gap.

'By the way,' he said, 'the notes you made on the bullfinches were most comprehensive. Absolute proof that my theory concerning the oriental tilberry trees was completely wrong.'

'Oh, I am sorry, Professor,' I told him.

'Not at all, dear boy,' said PB. 'As I've told you before, scientific theories must be tested if any progress is ever to be made. Now, take these bipedal water voles, for example—'

'Water voles?' I repeated. 'Bipedal?' I really didn't have time for this.

'Precisely, Barnaby. Precisely.' His face was flushed with excitement. 'I have recently noticed,' he said, 'that down by the river there are extremely unusual water-vole footprints that indicate the little creatures are learning to walk on their back legs.'

We turned into Wharf Street and continued on towards the theatre district.

'So that's what bipedal means, is it?' I asked, intrigued, despite myself.

'Indeed,' said the professor. 'My theory is that they are adapting their behaviour to the thick undergrowth of the riverside towpath – unusually tall, due to the recent fall in barge traffic—'

'And you'd like me to make observations?' I said.

'I would, Barnaby. I would,' he said, clapping his hands together. 'There are some excellent vantage points – high walls, tall overhanging trees – from which to observe the little creatures. And talking of creatures . . .' The professor reached into the pocket of his overcoat. 'Those rather singular specimens you presented me with the other week—'

'The hairs I found on Old Benjamin's chair?' I asked.

The professor nodded as he pulled a piece

of thick, creamy vellum, covered with spidery black symbols, numbers and words, from his pocket, and waved it in front of my nose.

'I examined them carefully and carried out various tests on the individual hairs,' he said. 'Tests which proved most interesting.' He paused for a moment, as if lost in thought.

He really had my attention now.

'Go on, PB,' I said. 'Interesting in what way?'

'Interesting,' said the professor, 'because all the evidence points to the fact that the hairs came from a lupine beast.'

'Lupine?' I said.

'A wolf, my dear boy,' Professor Pinkerton-Barnes explained. 'And an extremely large specimen at that. Rather unusual in the middle of a city, don't you think?'

'A wolf in the city.' My mind raced. 'Thank you, PB,' I said. 'You've been very helpful—'

'And does this mean that you'll help me out with my water-vole theory?' he asked.

I smiled. 'Of course,' I said. 'First thing Monday morning. In the meantime, there's something I need to check out for myself . . .'

We stopped outside a red-painted door with a brass knocker. 'Ah! My club,' smiled the professor. 'So good of you to stroll with me, dear chap.'

Calling 'goodnight' to the professor over my shoulder, I swiftly climbed the nearest drainpipe I could find – disturbing an indignant flock of roosting starlings as I did so. It was now quite dark, and as I arrived at the top, the full moon wobbled up above the horizon, huge and round and the colour of burnished gold.

'Beautiful,' I breathed. But then I remembered the last time I'd been on the rooftops when there was a full moon . . .

I began to make my way over the brick

firewalls and tiled roofs back towards Hartley Square and Dr Cadwallader's consulting rooms. I hadn't got far – the domed roof of the old Playhouse on the corner of Broad Street, to be precise – when I became aware of the sound of panic-filled screaming and shouting beneath me.

Dropping down onto the balcony below, I swung out on a jutting flagpole before taking a flying leap across to a tall pillar above the gas-lit theatre hoarding, which I slid down. Then, kneeling on the marble portico above the entrance to the Alhambra music hall, I peered down at the chaos gripping the streets.

There were men and women dashing this way and that, their eyes wide with fear. Children were wailing and sobbing, while all around, the sound of howling dogs echoed in the air.

'Hey, you!' I bellowed down to a theatre doorman standing below, a long pole held in his hands with which to defend himself.

He turned and looked up, his eyes wide with fright.

'What's going on?' I demanded.

'The constabulary's on its way!' he shouted back. 'Stay back! Clear the area! It's attacking anything in its path. Biting ... ripping out throats ...'

'What is?' I called.

His words chilled me to the bone.

'A wolf,' he gasped. 'A great black wolf!'

CHAPTER 10

The words had scarcely left the doorman's mouth when a great black beast sprang into the street from an alley just across from the theatre. Its blazing yellow eyes fixed on the luckless man, who brandished the wooden staff at it anxiously. All around, people scattered, screaming at the tops of their lungs. The huge black wolf's lustrous gleaming pelt rippled as its powerful muscles tensed and, in a flash of blurred movement, it leaped on its quarry.

There was a sickening crunch as the beast's mighty jaws closed on the man's neck and snapped it with a jerk of its head. The door-man's body crumpled to the ground directly beneath my vantage point up on the theatre hoarding, blood spurting from a gaping tear in his throat.

The black wolf threw back its head, its muzzle stained crimson with blood, and howled at the full moon. The hideous cry chilled me to the core of my being and left my heart hammering in my chest. It was unspeakably evil.

As the howl faded away, I found myself staring down into familiar glowing yellow eyes. Hadn't I witnessed the destruction of this hellhound in the vats of Greville's glue factory? Yet here it was before me, huge, black and bathed in blood. How was that possible? It was like a nightmare that, once dreamed, returns again and again to haunt the sleeper.

One thing was for certain, I realized as I crouched there: this creature did not come from the natural world . . .

All these thoughts and more raced through

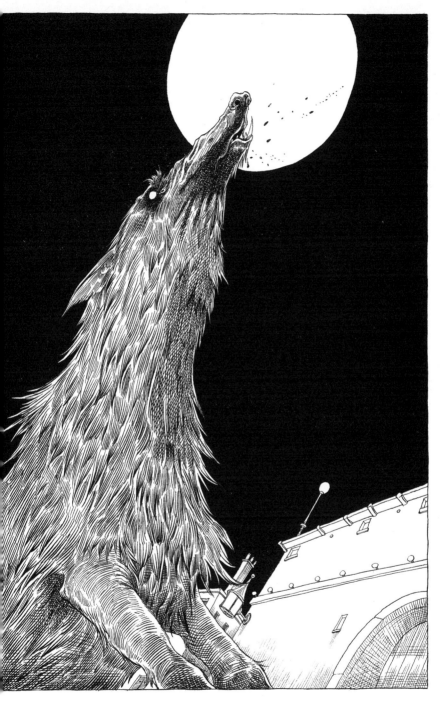

The great black wolf threw back its head, its muzzle stained crimson with blood, and howled at the full moon.

my mind as I gazed for those few terrifying seconds into the yellow eyes of the beast. Seeing it hesitate for a moment, I drew my swordstick and swung it at the nearest of the gaslights jutting out from the theatre hoarding.

The globe shattered and I stamped down hard on the exposed gas-fitting with my left foot, twisting it downwards. As I did so, a great spurt of flame flared from the broken gaslight onto the upturned muzzle of the wolf. It howled in alarm and, turning tail, fled off up a back street opposite. A moment later its huge black form disappeared into the stables at the back of the old Ambassador Theatre.

News of the wolf must have spread like a workhouse cough because, from the surrounding streets and out of every tavern and music hall of the theatre district, there came an unruly mob of toughs, swells and sightseers, armed with all manner of offensive weaponry – everything from curved bill-hooks to meat-cleavers and Saturday-night coshes. Soon the small alley was full to bursting with an angry, baying mob, brandishing burning torches and shouting boastful taunts as they clustered round the entrance to the stables.

Avoiding the naked flame of the gaslight, I swung down from the theatre hoarding and landed lightly on my feet on the pavement below. There was nothing I could do for the unfortunate doorman, whose lifeless body lay before me in a large pool of blood.

I crossed the street into the alley, which had become even more crowded with the arrival of the local constabulary clutching nets and police lanterns, followed closely by the district fire brigade, struggling with a large ladder. Now all we needed, I thought as I looked for a likely drainpipe to shin up, was a brass band and a carnival troupe or two, and we'd be all set for the wolf hunt!

As if in answer to my thoughts, a large woman just ahead of me turned – and I saw the tattoo of a mermaid in need of a shave on her large ham of a forearm. She was as white as a sheet of finest drawing paper. Even those tattoos of hers seemed paler than usual. A flicker of recognition passed across her face. I smiled.

'Barnaby,' she said, in a shaky voice. 'Barnaby Grimes. Come to see the show? They've got the terrible creature trapped in the old Ambassador's stables. Only one way in and one way out . . .'

'I know,' I told her. 'I saw it rip the throat out of the doorman at the Alhambra not five minutes ago.'

'I saw it, too!' she gasped. 'At the Sow's Ear! I was just going upstairs to wake Scaldy Sal – she had some appointment or other, and the stupid girl had overslept – when all hell broke loose in the attic rooms . . .'

She paused, her eyes watering and face

crumpling at the memory of it all. I pulled a handkerchief from a waistcoat pocket and handed it to her. She dabbed at her eyes, and swallowed hard.

'It must have got in from the rooftops. In a mad frenzy, it was,' she breathed, her voice little more than a stricken whisper. 'It raced down the stairs right past me and into the saloon bar, its evil yellow eyes blazing!'

Henrietta fanned herself with a large tattooed hand.

''Course, my regulars thought it was just another bar brawl. When it couldn't escape,' she said, swallowing again, 'the beast went mad. Started throwing itself at anyone in its path. Old Tom Brindel copped it first, throat torn out in an instant. Then Arnold Sellers. Never stood a chance . . .' She dabbed at her eyes again. 'Then young Albert Tomkins . . . Lovely lad, he was. A real gent . . . He copped it trying to save me . . .'

The tears were now running freely.

'Threw himself at the beast when it launched itself at the staircase where yours truly was standing, as transfixed as if I was back in the carnival sideshow!' she wept. 'But the wolf turned and savaged him like it was possessed. Bit through his neck. Blood gushing . . .'

'And then?' I said, giving her a moment to calm down.

'Then . . .' Henrietta said, in a flat voice, drained of emotion. 'Then it smashed through the saloon-bar window and ran off down the street . . .'

At that moment, above the din of the crowd, I became aware of another sound. I wasn't the only one, for a hush seemed to fall on the crowded alley as all eyes were fixed on the stable doors, from which the sound was coming.

It was bloodcurdling. The sound of whinnying horses in a blind panic mingled with horrific snarls and throaty roars. Even the boldest of the rough mob in the alley took a step back. I told Henrietta to keep my handkerchief, and found the drainpipe I'd been looking for.

Up on a nearby rooftop I had a better view of the chaos below. The fire brigade and police were jostling each other at the front of the mob, clearly at a loss to know what to do. None of them wanted to be the first to enter the stables, whose great wooden doors stood tantalizingly ajar.

From inside the stable – the noise amplified by its size – the terrible sounds seemed to be reaching some hideous crescendo. The screams of the horses and snarls of the trapped beast grew so loud, so disturbing, that some of the crowd put their hands over their ears to cut it out.

Suddenly a high-pitched shriek of absolute fury and terror cut through the air. It was followed, moments later, by a reverberating *crash!* – and a huge grey carthorse, twenty hands high, burst out of the stables and through the scattering crowd. For a moment there was blind panic as the terrified horse – horribly mauled and bleeding – trampled several firemen in its path and disappeared off into Strap Street.

When some sort of order was restored, all eyes turned once more to the stable doors, now hanging off their hinges. Inside the shadowy interior there was an eerie silence, perhaps more appalling than the sounds that had preceded it.

Nobody spoke. Nobody moved.

Below me, a constable with a short carbine and police lantern stepped forward and gingerly entered the stables. He was followed by several more, half of whom exited at once and brought up the remains of their supper noisily in the gutter outside.

'It's not here,' a voice announced from inside the stables.

A groan went round the crowd.

'Then where is it?' someone demanded.

'What's happened to it?'

'No idea,' the first voice replied. 'But it's not here. Disappeared into thin air . . .'

'It must have found another way out. Dug through the floor, perhaps?' someone suggested.

'Or climbed up and escaped over the rooftops?'

I knew this was impossible as I would have seen the creature if it had taken to the high stacks, but nevertheless, the suggestion made my blood run cold. With a shiver, I climbed down from the rooftop and entered the stable behind a few other onlookers with strong stomachs.

To this day, I wish I hadn't. The sight of six fine coach horses ripped to pieces in their stalls is one I never want to see again. The bitter taste of bile rose in my throat as I looked around the slaughterhouse that the old Ambassador's stables had become.

Suddenly a voice rang out from the corner. 'Over here!'

'What is it?'

'A body . . .'

I made my way across the blood-soaked floor of the stables. Sure enough, lying on the floor was a body. It looked as if its neck was broken, and there was the bloody wound from a carthorse hoof on its temple.

'Does anyone know this person?' a constable was asking.

Around me, everyone shook their heads. Yet as the flickering torchlight fell across the body, and I saw the black hair, the thin lips and bulbous nose – the angry skin, blistered, flaking and the colour of a strawberry – I knew that I did.

It was Scaldy Sal.

CHAPTER 11

By the time I'd taken a near-hysterical Henrietta back to the Sow's Ear and helped her to clear up the shattered furniture and broken bottles, not to mention mopping down the floors – and earned her undying gratitude in the process – the night had passed.

As the sun rose over the rooftops, I returned to my rooms. I was tired. Dog-tired. I made my way wearily along the roof gutter to the window of my attic and stepped inside.

The terrible events of the night before . . . the murderous beast, the mayhem in the streets and, most of all, Scaldy Sal's dead eyes staring up at me. It hardly seemed real

– yet already, the headlines of the first editions were being shouted out by the early-morning newspaper sellers in the streets below.

'*Wolf runs amok! Five dead in hellhound horror!*'

I kicked off my boots and crawled under my quilt – the oriental one the captain of the *Jade Dragon* had given me after the shocking incident of the temple demon . . .

As my head hit the pillow, I was out like a watchman's brazier in a hailstorm. Not that it did me any good.

My dreams were full of blazing yellow eyes, bared fangs and dead doormen. I was highstacking over the rooftops, pursued by a whole pack of hellhounds, their fetid breath hot on my collar, when I made a wild leap for a chimney I never should have attempted. Sure enough, down I went. Falling, falling into blackness, until the scabby red face of Scaldy Sal came looming up at me—

I awoke with a start, dripping with sweat and tangled up in my bedclothes. Shafts of bright afternoon sunlight broke through a gap in the shutters and sliced through my cluttered rooms.

'It was just a dream,' I said out loud. 'It's over now.'

Yet even as I uttered the words, I knew they weren't true. It wasn't a dream – and it was very far from over!

I climbed from my bed, splashed water over my face and got dressed. With the terror and confusion of the previous night, I hadn't had a chance to spy on Dr Cadwallader's consulting rooms. I shook my head. I knew, with a cold chill in my heart, what I had to do now.

Without further ado, I highstacked over to Bradstock and Clink's chambers, entering through an open window on the fourth floor, and descended the stairs to the two gentlemen's offices. I knocked.

'Enter!' came a voice.

'Ah, Barnaby,' said Mr Bradstock as I walked into the chambers. 'Come in, come in . . .'

'Has Mr Clink stepped out?' I said, hoping against hope as I spotted the empty desk on the other side of the window from the younger lawyer's.

'No, Barnaby,' he replied. 'And it's most unusual. Mr Clink hasn't come in to chambers this morning.'

My heart sank.

He nodded across to the desk opposite. It was tidy, with the quills sharpened and laid out in a neat row, the inkpots filled and stoppered, and a clean blotter in place. The old man was obviously in the habit of preparing his desk for the following day. This morning, however, the tools of his trade were clearly untouched.

'I don't understand it at all,' Mr Bradstock was saying. 'Forty-seven years he's been working at that very desk – long before I ever started here – and he's never missed a single day's work in his life. Even when he was troubled by those aches and pains of his, he would be here at eight o'clock on the dot. You could set your timepiece by him, Barnaby. I can't think what could have happened to him.' He shook his head. 'Surely he can't be ill. I mean, he's been so fit and healthy lately, ever since—'

'He started taking Doctor Cadwallader's cordial,' I broke in.

'Precisely.' He nodded, then paused. 'I don't suppose you could look in on him at his house . . . ? I can give you his address—'

'No need,' I said, patting my waist-coat pocket. 'I have Mr Clink's address already.'

'You have?' said Mr Bradstock.

'Yes,' I said, my mind racing. 'And I'd be happy to check on him.'

'Thank you, Barnaby!' said Mr Bradstock,

shaking my hand vigorously. 'It would set my mind at rest!'

Back up on the rooftops, I took a moment to survey the filth and grandeur of the city all around me. The sooty rooftops of the Wasps' Nest, where Mr Clink lived, and the tall elegant spires of the financial district. I turned and headed off in a different direction completely. If I was to stand any chance of finding Mr Clink, I knew where to start looking . . .

Twenty minutes later, with the sun already sinking in the sky, I was balancing my way along the line of ridge tiles at the top of the curving row of houses that formed Hartley Square. At number 27 I paused, clambered over the sloping roof and peered down through the skylight I had just noticed.

On closer inspection, the skylight was shut tight. What was more, some sort of mechanical shutters inside made it impossible to see in.

Strange, I thought as I made my way down from the roof. A skylight that shuts out light . . .

I shinned down the drainpipe and dropped lightly to the ground. I was just checking for lurking policemen before turning the corner and approaching the front door when it opened. And who should emerge but Ellen Wicks, the pretty shop girl. Only today, I noticed, her face was pale and pinched, and her eyes had a haunted, frightened look about them.

She and the second attendant I'd seen before were carrying a large packing case between them, staggering awkwardly down the steps to a waiting carriage. I would have given them a hand if it hadn't been for their employer, Madame Scutari. She came bustling out after them, waving her umbrella and insisting that Ellen 'be careful with the merchandise' and 'look lively and wipe that expression off your face, my girl. I don't know where he gets them from, but where else are we to get such quality? You tell me that!'

The packing case was bundled inside the carriage and the three of them disappeared in a cloud of dust, cracked whips and cries to the coachman of 'Faster! Faster! We've got customers waiting!'

I turned the corner, was let into the building by the concierge and made my way up the flights of stairs to the top floor.

'Ah, Mr Grimes,' said Dr Cadwallader somewhat distractedly when he opened the door to see yours truly standing there. 'Come in and wait for me in my study. I've just got a little matter to attend to.'

The little matter, it seemed, was a great wad of banknotes bulging in the inside pocket of his white coat – banknotes which still bore the faint but unmistakable whiff of Madame Scutari's perfume.

I went through to the doctor's study, with

its large desk and leather chairs, and sat down. Dr Cadwallader disappeared into the room beyond, leaving the door ajar. Silently I got up, tiptoed across the floor and peered in.

The room was dark, and seemed to be padded. It smelled strongly of carbolic soap, which masked an underlying odour of pickling solution. It was quite empty, apart from a large hook which hung from the padded ceiling just next to the shuttered skylight I'd seen from outside. The doctor was in the corner of the chamber, packing his wad of banknotes into a wall safe, chuckling delightedly to himself.

I returned to my chair, but not before noticing the doctor's medical bag – the one with the initials N.J.W. in faded gold letters – standing beside the desk. Glancing back furtively at the padded chamber, I knelt down and opened the bag.

Nestling inside were six glass and chrome

syringes, each one with a plunger at one end and a long needle-point glinting at the other. Then I noticed something else. Five of the six had been used. The plungers had been depressed and the contents expelled, presumably injected into the arms of the good doctor's patients. The sixth syringe, however, remained unused. The plunger was out as far as it would go and the glass tube was full of a thick silvery-white substance—

Just then, from the padded chamber behind me, I heard the wall safe click shut. Quickly I pulled a handkerchief from my jacket pocket and wrapped it around the needle of the sixth syringe, before slipping it into the deepest pocket of my poacher's waistcoat.

I just had time to regain my chair when the doctor stepped back into the room – only to silently curse my carelessness a moment later. I had left the medical bag open beside the desk. Luckily Dr Cadwallader didn't seem to notice. He was relaxed and happy; probably still thinking of the fortune in banknotes nestling in that safe of his. He sat down in the chair opposite and adjusted his pince-nez.

'Now, what can I do for you, Mr Grimes?' he asked, his eyes narrowed.

'I've got some bad news, Doctor,' I said. 'It's about one of your patients. Sarah Monahan. She was killed last night, and in the most terrible circumstances—'

'Killed?' The doctor stopped smiling and his eyes narrowed. 'I wondered what had happened to her when she failed to keep her appointment. Killed, you say?'

'She was caught up in all the mayhem in the theatre district last night,' I said, 'and it appears she was kicked in the head by a horse. They found her body in the old Ambassador's stables.'

The doctor breathed in noisily. 'Yes, yes, the wolf attack. I read about it in this morning's paper. Most regrettable,' he muttered. 'Most regrettable, indeed. Poor Sarah. My cordial had done her the power of good, restored her to exceptional health ... I was so looking forward to our last appointment. Still,' he said, and shrugged, 'I suppose it can't be helped.'

'There is just *one* other thing,' I said, looking up.

'Yes?' said the doctor, smiling once more.

'Aloysius Clink,' I said. 'An old client of mine. He didn't come in to work this morning.'

'What is this to me?' Dr Cadwallader demanded.

'He is a patient of yours, Doctor. I delivered your letter to him. He's a lawyer – quite wealthy, by all accounts. You know him as Mr Klynkowiczski.'

The doctor's right eyebrow shot up. He fixed me with a dark look. 'A wealthy lawyer, you say? But he looked like an old tramp.

Lived in that slum you call . . . the Wasps' Nest, is it?'

'His family home,' I said. 'Mr Clink – I mean, Klynkowiczski doesn't bother much about his outward appearance. But he is one of the finest lawyers in the city—'

'Mr Klynkowiczski did visit me last night,' Dr Cadwallader broke in. 'I gave him his final treatment and then he left, completely cured.' He frowned. 'Come to think of it, he did say something about taking a trip – to the coast, if my memory serves me well . . .'

'A trip to the coast?' I said. 'That doesn't sound like Mr Clink—'

For a second time the doctor interrupted me. 'My dear Mr Grimes,' he said. 'When a patient's course of treatment has been completed, I wish them a long and healthy life, and take them off my list. But if I'd known this Mr Clink of yours was a wealthy lawyer, I'd never have agreed to give him my cordial in the first place.'

'You wouldn't?'

'Of course not, Mr Grimes.' The doctor adjusted his pince-nez and fixed me with those steel-grey eyes of his. 'My cordial is for the poor and needy, the downtrodden and easily overlooked. But then, having delivered my reminders, Mr Grimes,' – he shot me a wolfish grin – 'you should know that all too well.'

I smiled back as casually as I could, and rose to go. 'You are a true philanthropist, Doctor,' I told him.

'I shall need your services again the same time next month, Mr Grimes,' he said. 'I trust I can rely on you.'

'You certainly can, Doctor Cadwallader,' I said, though as I left his consulting rooms, I knew that I'd be seeing Dr Cadwallader far sooner than that. Only when I did, he wouldn't be seeing me . . .

Over the next week or so I followed the

good doctor everywhere. From up on the rooftops I watched his every move as he ventured into the poorer parts of the city, stopping and chatting to everyone he met. Some he seemed to dismiss after a moment's conversation. Others he spent hours with, listening to their stories of ill-health and misfortune. Standing on a ledge or concealed in a doorway, I listened as the doctor set to work.

'Such misfortune, my dear,' I heard him say to an old washerwoman in Slaughterhouse Lane. 'And no one to look after you?'

'No, no,' I heard the old woman saying, her voice weak and faltering. 'Not a single person in the world. Live on me own, I do. Always have done – well, ever since my Alfie died . . .'

'And that, of course, must make every-thing even more difficult for you,' the doctor said, his voice low and solicitous. 'Do you not have neighbours who could help you out? Friends, perhaps? Relatives?'

'I've told you, Doctor Cadwallader, sir,' she said. 'There's no one.'

'Well, I think that's very sad,' the doctor said, and from my hiding place, halfway up the wall in the adjacent alley, I saw him open his bag and remove one of his blue bottles of cordial. 'You give me your address, Lily Wagstaff, my dear,' he said, 'and I'll give you one of my special cordials. You're to take a spoonful of it every day for the next three weeks, then come along to my surgery for your final treatment . . .' He smiled. 'I'll send you a reminder.'

'That's very kind of you,' said Lily, 'but I can't afford it, Doctor. I struggle to make ends meet as it is, what with the washing and my bad back—'

'Oh, I don't want payment,' he said with a smile. 'It's enough for me to know I've helped out someone as deserving as your good self.'

He noted her address in his little black book, tipped his hat and went on his way.

The second bottle of Dr Cadwallader's cordial went to a toothless rag-and-bone man he encountered scouring the streets with his horse and cart on the east side of the city. A widower with neither brothers nor sisters, sons nor daughters, he was only too happy to try the free tonic which the doctor assured him – pointing to the words on the label as he spoke – was 'an efficacious elixir for the enhancement of mental and physical powers . . .'

'I don't know about the mental stuff,' the man laughed. 'Never been that gifted in this department,' he said, tapping his finger to his temple. 'Not like your good self, Doctor. But it'd certainly be a treat to have some of those there physical powers you speak of.'

'My pleasure, Mr Lester,' smiled the doctor. 'My pleasure, indeed!'

Lily Wagstaff and Ed Lester were soon

followed by Eliza Hunter, Victoria Draper, Molly Suggs and a tall, stooped undertaker by the name of Ferdinand Cripps.

I returned to Hartley Square the day after Dr Cadwallader had presented Mr Cripps with his cordial, and the day after that. And, for good measure, the day after that as well. But the doctor made no further trips to the Wasps' Nest, to the Eastern Quay or any of the other poorer areas of the city – which was just as well, because I needed time to prepare for what lay ahead.

For a start, as well as my usual work there was the important research I'd undertaken at Underhill's Library for Scholars of the Arcane; research which was proving very interesting. Also, there were some extremely complex experiments I had got PB working on, which involved me running all over town buying up patent medicines by the sackful . . .

It was in the middle of the night before

my next – and what I intended to be my last – assignment for Dr Cadwallader when I heard the professor's voice ring out.

'By Gad, I think I've got it!'

The pair of us were up in his laboratory. I was dozing on the couch. I'd been reading through the most recent notes I'd taken in the library, trying to piece together the bits of information before I dropped off. Meanwhile, the professor had been stooped over a tangled mass of interlinked glass flasks, copper pots, bell jars and test tubes, a teat-pipette clutched in his hands, adding a drop of a yellowish liquid into the bubbling test tube in front of him.

'Are you sure?' I asked, leaping up from the couch.

'As sure as I can be, Barnaby,' he said, holding up a small vial of dark-green liquid to the light. 'Now, according to my theory, the photo-lycanthropic susceptibilities can be blocked at the sub-folic level quite effectively with an orally delivered solution . . .'

As I listened to the professor describe the intricacies of the experiment he'd been working on, I found myself hoping against hope that this was one theory that would prove to be right . . .

The following day I highstacked across the city to Hartley Square, presenting myself to Dr Cadwallader at seven o'clock on the dot.

'Punctual as usual, Mr Grimes,' he said, his eyes twinkling. 'I have the envelopes here waiting for you.'

I thanked him and, thrusting the six letters into a pocket of my poacher's waistcoat, took my leave of the good doctor.

I climbed back onto the rooftops and made my way across the city until I'd put a reasonable distance between myself and Hartley Square. Then, stopping beside a small crenellated turret, I sat down and pulled out the letters Dr Cadwallader had given me. As I had suspected, the names were all familiar.

Lily Wagstaff. Ed Lester. Eliza Hunter. Victoria Draper. Molly Suggs. Ferdinand Cripps.

I looked at their addresses and copied them down. Dilapidated hovels in rundown streets, all of them. Then, my heart thumping beneath my waistcoat, I did what I had never done before – what no tick-tock lad worth his salt would ever do intentionally.

I tore them up.

The envelopes, together with the letters they contained ... Tear after tear, turning them bit by bit into a thousand tiny scraps of paper which I cupped in my hand and, standing on the very edge of the building, threw to the wind. They fluttered down, like feathers over a grouse moor.

Then, sitting down once more, I pulled out six new envelopes, together with six hand-

They fluttered down, like feathers over a grouse moor.

written cards, from the inside of my jacket, along with six glass vials of the dark-green tincture. I put a card and one of the small stoppered bottles into each of the envelopes, and copied out the names and addresses onto the front. Then I set off for the first of my six drops.

Lily Wagstaff seemed to be expecting me. 'You've come from that nice Doctor Cadwallader, haven't you?' she said.

I told her I had.

'I've got to tell you, that doctor, he's a miracle worker,' she said, her face creasing up in a great big grin. 'Never felt so good in all my born days.'

I handed her the envelope.

'Ooh, read it for me, there's a good lad,' she said. 'I never was good with words myself.'

I opened the envelope and took out the card: '*Find enclosed your final treatment.*' I handed her the small bottle.

'Please take immediately. Your appointment has been cancelled,' I read as Lily
Wagstaff unstoppered the bottle and drank
its contents. 'Doctor Cadwallader is unwell.'

CHAPTER 12

*D*r Cadwallader was no fool. He'd made sure he was well connected. He'd ingratiated himself with the chief constable, and taken on Madame Scutari – the mayor's cousin – as a business partner. So long as he was discreet and kept his evil deals confined to the poorest quarters of the city, he believed that he was untouchable.

Well I, for one, wasn't going to stand for it. Never mind the chief constable, the mayor or Madame Scutari; this was *my* city and I was going to protect it! I intended to confront Dr Cadwallader with what I knew, and if he refused to pack his bags and leave that very night, I was going to shout his dirty secret from the rooftops if necessary.

And when it comes to rooftops, as I'm sure you realize by now, I know a thing or two. Nevertheless, it was with a sense of foreboding that I made my way back to Hartley Square that evening as the sun sank low in the sky.

'Ah, Mr Grimes, I'm pleased to see you,' Dr Cadwallader said, smiling as he opened the door to his consulting rooms and ushered me in. 'I must say, I was getting a little concerned. It is almost sunset and yet none of my patients have presented themselves for their final treatments. You did deliver my reminders, I trust?'

I shook my head.

'*No*, Mr Grimes?' The smile froze on his face, then faded slowly, to be replaced with an altogether grimmer expression. 'No?'

'We need to talk,' I said.

'So it seems, Mr Grimes,' said Dr

Cadwallader, a hint of steel in his voice. 'Come through to my office. We shall discuss matters there.'

I followed the doctor through the waiting room. The six red chairs with the gold piping and tassels had been pulled away from the walls and stood now in a convivial circle, in anticipation of the patients who were to have arrived. The periodicals had been cleared from the small table. Instead, there was a lacquered tray upon it, laid out with six teacups. We went through to his office.

'Sit down, Mr Grimes,' said Dr Cadwallader.

I did so.

'Now,' he said, 'perhaps you'd like to tell me what is going on.'

'I rather hoped, Doctor Cadwallader,' I said, keeping my voice calm and steady, 'you'd like to tell *me*.'

The doctor hesitated, his steel-grey eyes staring intently into mine from behind his tinted pince-nez as if trying to read my thoughts. Then he smiled. 'Quite so, Mr Grimes,' he said. 'But first, a nice cup of tea?'

I nodded. The doctor picked up a silver teapot from the tray on his desk and motioned for me to fetch some teacups. I took two from the tray in the waiting room and returned. I don't quite know what I'd been expecting. A violent rage? An angry tirade? Denials and threats? But if the doctor wanted to be civilized about this, then that was fine by me.

Smiling, he poured the steaming tea into the two cups. 'Milk?' he said. 'Sugar?'

I said yes to both.

'Now, Mr Grimes,' he said smoothly as he stirred the tea and set the steaming cup down before me, 'what exactly seems to be the problem?'

'The problem, Doctor,' I began, as calmly as I could, 'is that your patients have a nasty habit of disappearing.'

The doctor shrugged. 'When they finish their treatment, they are no longer my concern, Mr Grimes.'

'Really, Doctor?' I said. 'Then what about Sarah Monahan? Or Scaldy Sal. Found dead in a place where a wolf had run amok . . . The same type of creature that I myself confronted on the night of Old Benjamin's disappearance – another of your patients, Doctor.'

The doctor's steel-grey eyes bored into mine.

'But then, as you know all too well, Doctor Cadwallader, sightings of wolves in cities are nothing new.'

I paused, leaned forward and took the cup of tea in my hand – and sniffed it.

The doctor shot me a knowing grin. 'You are too clever for me, Mr Grimes,' he said, removing his pince-nez. 'The tea is indeed drugged. I find it helps to sedate my patients before their final transformation.'

'I have done some research, Doctor Cadwallader,' I said in measured tones as I replaced the cup on its saucer. 'Or should I say, Doctor Klaus – or, more properly, *Niklaus* Johannes Westphale, werewolf hunter?'

I tightened my grip on my swordstick, but the doctor continued to smile.

'N.J.W.,' I said. 'The initials on that medical bag of yours.'

'Yes, yes, Mr Grimes,' he said. 'I am indeed Doctor Westphale.' He leaned forward in his chair and spread his long, thin fingers on the desk in front of him. His face looked pale and drawn. 'I spent my life ridding the world of werewolves, hunting them down, destroying them . . . And what thanks did I get?' He grimaced angrily. 'A tiny pension and the fear and contempt of my fellow man. Finally I fell ill, and so I did what I'd done all my life.' He slammed a gnarled fist down on the desk. 'I fought back. I experimented; refining and distilling – until I found a cure . . .'

'Your cordial?' I said, my mouth dry.

'My cordial.' The doctor nodded. 'Distilled from the saliva of a werewolf, my dear Mr Grimes. It bestowed a savage animal energy and boundless vitality, which to this day, almost a century later, endures – but at a cost. Whoever takes it risks turning into a werewolf if struck by the rays of the full moon. An unfortunate side effect, but one I turned to my advantage. I faked my death and went out into the world all those years ago to profit from my amazing discovery.'

I shook my head angrily. I thought of Scaldy Sal, and how brave she'd been after her terrible furnace accident. And of Tom Garrick and Scobie Rathbone – good, solid individuals, grateful that someone had treated them well, easing their aches and pains, both so wickedly betrayed. And of course Old Benjamin, the retired coachman who had been such a good friend to me all my life . . .

'I found the weak, the poor, the vulnerable – those who wouldn't be missed – and I gave them my cordial. Then I invited them back on the following full moon for a final injection—'

'The syringe,' I interrupted. 'Tincture of mercury and deadly nightshade.'

The doctor smiled. 'You *have* done your research. I'm impressed, Mr Grimes. I was a werewolf hunter – the greatest there has ever been. I know all there is to know about killing the lycanthrope. Yet my fixing solution is my greatest discovery – even greater than my cordial. It kills werewolves "in fur", the victims never regaining their human form.' The doctor rubbed his hands together delightedly. 'As I said, Mr Grimes, I turned the unfortunate side effects to my advantage.'

I shuddered. 'You skin them, Doctor, and sell their pelts as—'

'Westphalian trim,' the doctor cackled, his

right arm whipping up from the desk.

I felt a sharp pain and, looking down, saw a feather-flighted dart embedded in my shoulder.

'Drugged tea.' The doctor laughed. 'My dear Mr Grimes, there is more than one way to skin a wolf.'

Wolf . . . Wolf . . . Wolf . . .

The words echoed in my head as I tried in vain to climb out of my chair and draw my swordstick. The whole room was blurred and swimming. My body felt both numb and incredibly heavy. There was a loud buzzing noise inside my head, then . . .

Nothing.

I don't know how long I was unconscious for, but when I came round, I was lying on the padded floor of the doctor's laboratory. I looked around groggily – at the quilted walls, at the glinting hook high above my head.

'You surprise me, Mr Grimes.'

It was the doctor's voice, and it was coming from the far side of the laboratory. Straining every fibre of my body, I turned my head. And there he was, over by the wall. He was wearing a white surgical smock and long rubber gloves. In his hands was a huge syringe, which he was holding up as he measured off the silvery-white contents against the calibrations. He turned and smiled thinly.

'I expected you to put up more of a fight.'

I said nothing. But inside, my stomach churned and my head screamed. How stupid I'd been! I should have skewered him with my swordstick first and asked questions after. Instead, I was now at the doctor's mercy.

He turned and came towards me, pushing his pince-nez up his nose as he advanced.

'Apologies for the crude manner in which I had to administer the cordial,' he added. 'My patients usually have a three-week course, but in your case, Mr Grimes—'

'My case?' I rasped – and as I spoke, I realized how raw and bruised my throat felt.

The doctor nodded towards the three empty blue bottles lying beside me, as well as the funnel and length of rubber tubing.

'I had to give you an especially concentrated dose, you see,' he said. 'Just to be on the safe side.'

I wanted to leap to my feet, but I couldn't move a muscle. The lingering effects of the drugged dart were just too strong.

'Now' – he smiled down at me – 'shall we apply the *final* treatment?'

With those words, he turned and pulled a huge hood with sinister dark glass panels for eyes down over his head. Then, reaching up, he grabbed a thick cord that hung down from the skylight, and pulled. There was a click and a creak. Slowly but surely, the slatted shutters above my head began to open. As they did so, they revealed the great white sphere of the full moon. It shone down, bathing me in a pool of silvery light.

Have you ever felt your skin being peeled slowly away from your arms and legs? Your muscles being torn and shredded as every bone in your body fights to burst through your flesh? Every tendon and sinew stretched to breaking point as your skeleton attempts to rip itself apart from the inside?

That is what it feels like to turn into a werewolf. And it is something I'll never forget so long as I live.

My fingers and toes lengthened and transformed themselves into hard, claw-tipped paws. My neck strained, my belly cramped, my muscles knotted and rippled. Suddenly my tongue – long and glistening – was lolling from the corner of my mouth, as my nose and jaw lengthened into a snarling snout, which bared to reveal drooling fangs. And, as I writhed and squirmed in a torment of pain, from every part of my body there sprouted thick, lustrous, dark-brown fur . . .

'Aaah-ooo-ooo!' I cried, despite myself, throwing back my head and howling at the moon.

When I looked down, I saw the doctor's syringe glint in the moonlight – the syringe that bore the tincture of mercury and nightshade that would kill me. All at once it all became horribly clear.

I would be hung from the hook, like all those others before me whose splattered blood still stained the pale-grey padded walls. I would be skinned from top to toe, and my pelt would be sold to Madame Scutari, no questions asked, to be turned into a sought-after fur collar or cuff for a wealthy customer: the celebrated Westphalian trim.

No, I told myself, fighting to regain the vestiges of the human being I had once been. *I refuse to become an animal!*

Summoning all the strength I could muster from the very depths of my being, I tensed my muscles as the sinister figure of the doctor approached me, the deadly syringe grasped in his hand.

Closer . . . Closer . . .

All at once, with a curdling howl, I sprang at the doctor, knocking him backwards. We hit the floor with a loud *thud*. The doctor let go of the syringe, which bounced away across the padded floor.

To this day, I don't quite know what came over me – but I was a wolf, and in danger, and I reacted like any cornered animal would. I went for the doctor's throat. What I got was a mouthful of thick cotton-like gauze that made up the doctor's hood, which I tore off with a flick of my neck.

For a moment I found myself glaring down into those steel-grey eyes as they glinted in the moonlight. They stared back at me, the absolute terror clear in their gaze.

'No,' the doctor moaned. 'No . . . No, no, no . . .' His voice was loud and crazed. '*No!*'

He twisted round and stared up at the white disc of the full moon, his face contorted with fear . . .

'N-aaah ooo-ooo!' His voice broke, switching at that moment from a human cry of anguish to a terrible wolf-like howl.

At the same instant his body began to buckle and convulse. I saw his limbs flex and his muscles writhe, as if he'd been struck by a bolt of lightning. The doctor was going through the selfsame transformation that I had just endured.

By my reckoning, Klaus Johannes Westphale was over one hundred and fifty years old, kept youthful and vigorous by the use of his accursed cordial. Unlike his unfortunate patients, though, he'd always been at great pains to protect himself from the rays of the full moon. Now his luck had run out.

As I watched, horrified, I saw his fingers elongate and curl, and the nails harden to savage claws. I saw his spine arch and bend backwards; his jaw lengthen and sprout glinting fangs. And as this hideous trans-formation took place, deep, guttural sounds rumbled in his throat, becoming less human and more bestial by the second.

And then, as I stood transfixed and rooted to the spot, his clothes split and his body began to sprout fur. Thick, glossy and as white as pure, driven snow, it appeared all over his wolf-like body. Up his limbs and across his back it went, growing especially long and luxuriant up the curve of his neck. Over his ears, round his eyes and down the snout to his teeth – which were bared and snarling and full of hatred . . .

With a blood-curdling cry, the hellish creature that the doctor had become pounced, knocking me hard against the padded wall of the chamber. For a moment I was stunned and winded, but only for a moment. The next, I swerved out of reach of the white

With a blood-curdling cry, the hellish creature pounced…

wolf's glinting fangs and spun round, my own bared teeth snarling menacingly as the fur at my neck and down my back stood on end.

A dark surge of unspeakable fury welled up in me. I didn't just want to kill the white wolf circling round me, its fangs glinting, its piercing grey eyes narrowed to evil slits as it sized up my throat; I wanted to tear it limb from limb, claw my way into its innards and rip its entrails out with my bare fangs.

With an ear-splitting screech, the snow-white beast flew towards me, claws outstretched and slavering jaws agape. I launched myself back at it. Suddenly we were entwined in a savage, snarling, snapping embrace. A red blur filled my vision as my animal limbs coursed with a supernatural energy. My jaws bit and tore as my talons flashed and clawed. We thudded against the padded walls and floor in a blind frenzy of hatred and rage.

All at once the white wolf let out a piercing yowl of pain, so loud I reeled back across the floor. For a moment all I could see was stars shooting, but when the shock waves cleared and my eyes focused once more, I saw the white wolf lying slumped and motionless across the chamber from me.

Slowly, cautiously, my tail lowered and, neck hair on end, I crossed the floor. I lowered my head and sniffed . . .

The deadly syringe was sticking out of the white wolf's arched back, the plunger compressed, the glass cylinder emptied.

A fierce animal surge of triumph coursed through my powerful body. I threw back my head and howled at the moon.

Strange as the events of that night were, the events of the morning after were stranger still. When I came to my human senses, I was naked in a padded chamber containing a very big and very dead white wolf. The early dawn light confirmed that I had resumed my human form, just like poor Scaldy Sal before me, only I was lucky enough to have lived to tell the tale.

Not that I felt particularly lucky at that moment. My head ached and every muscle in my body felt as if it had been beaten with a meat-tenderizer. Still, I was able to pull on the doctor's overcoat, which I found hanging on his office door, the feel of its Westphalian trim making me shudder; pick up my ripped poacher's waistcoat, my swordstick and hat, and get out of there.

My first drop that morning was at the third-floor laboratory of Professor Pinkerton-Barnes. I told him of the horrors of the night before; my stupidity in allowing the doctor to get the better of me and his terrible fate. PB assured me that the other victims of the doctor were all safe and well, and that I would be too. Though, as he pressed the small bottle of dark-green tincture into my hand – the result of many long hours in the laboratory – I still had my doubts.

As I drained the bottle to its dregs, all I could do was pray that PB's discovery – following his endless testing of innumerable patent medicines – was indeed correct.

I needn't have bothered, for that evening, as I stood at the open window of my attic rooms beneath the silvery glow of the full moon, I was as smooth and hairless as a newborn baby, thanks to the remarkable hair-loss associated with Old Mother Berkeley's Patent Tonic!

I wish I could say that the horrors of the previous night were as easily banished, but I cannot. The memory of my terrible transformation still haunts me. But worse even than that is the memory conjured up when a coach-and-four rattles past me in the street. Then a wave of unbearable sadness fills me as I remember Old Benjamin and his terrible fate.

Poor Old Benjamin, transformed into a werewolf as he sat in his coachman's chair. That night he had sought out the beguiling moonlight up on the rooftops, where I, his friend, killed him.

Could I have done any different? Perhaps – I don't know. That question is the most terrible one of all.

As for the doctor, well, I'm tempted to say I never saw hide nor hair of him again. But that would be a lie.

His consulting rooms were cleared out by his business partner, Madame Scutari, and the whole sordid mess hushed up by her cousin, the mayor. Not that the elegant madame had ever asked questions. She had just taken the furs that the good doctor supplied her with – and was happy to do so.

When her supply dried up, so too did the demand for Westphalian trim. The well-to-do fashionable crowd deserted Madame

Scutari's shop in droves and she went out of business.

Serves her right, I say!

The good news was that I was able to introduce the pretty Ellen to an enterprising dressmaker in Taplow Square, where she soon made her name anticipating the latest thing. A season later, the ladies of Gallop Row and Regency Mall had moved on to Japanese silk and jasmine corsages ...

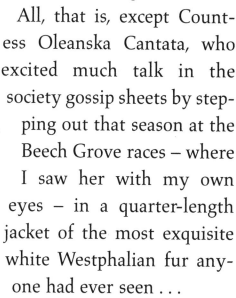

All, that is, except Countess Oleanska Cantata, who excited much talk in the society gossip sheets by stepping out that season at the Beech Grove races – where I saw her with my own eyes – in a quarter-length jacket of the most exquisite white Westphalian fur anyone had ever seen ...

PAUL STEWART & CHRIS RIDDELL

BARNABY GRIMES

RETURN of the EMERALD SKULL

Turn the page for an exclusive peek at
the first chapter of the new Barnaby Grimes
book, in stores spring 2009.

CHAPTER

1

'Cut out his beating heart,' the ancient voice commanded, each syllable dripping with a dark evil that I was powerless to resist.

Overhead, the moon slid slowly but inexorably across the face of the sun, casting the courtyard into a dreadful dusk. And as the light faded, so did the last vestiges of my will to resist. There was nothing that I could do.

A circle of shadowy figures clustered around the great slab that lay before me, like a flock of hideous vultures. Their beaked faces and long, rustling feathers quivered with awful anticipation as their dark eye-sockets turned, as one, towards me.

On awkward, stumbling legs, I approached the wooden altar like a sleepwalker, climbing one step after the other, powerless to resist.

The hideous figures parted as I drew closer. At the altar, I looked down. There, stripped to the waist, lying face-up and spread-eagled, was a man, roped into place. There were cuts and weals on his skin – some scabbed over, some fresh – and his ribs were sticking up, giving his chest the appearance of a damaged glockenspiel.

His head lolled to one side and, from his parted lips, there came a low, rasping moan.

'Please,' he pleaded, gazing up at me with the panic-stricken eyes of a ferret-cornered rabbit. 'Don't do it, I'm begging you…'

At that moment, the final dazzling rays of the sun were extinguished by the dark orb of the moon. In shock, I looked up into the sky. The whole disc had turned pitch black and from the circumference of the circle, a spiky ring of light streamed out in all directions, like a black merciless eye staring down from the heavens.

The tallest of the feathered figures stepped forward to face me. It wore a great crown of iridescent blue plumage. Behind him, nestling like a grotesque egg on the cushion of a high-backed leather chair, was a hideous grinning skull. As I stared, the huge jewels in the skull's eye-sockets started to glow a bright and bloody crimson, which stained the eerie twilight of the eclipse.

The feathered figure reached into its cape and withdrew a large stone knife, which it held out to me. Again the ancient voice rasped in my head.

'Cut out his beating heart!'

Despite myself, I reached out and gripped the haft of the stone knife in my hands. As I did so, I felt my arm being raised up into the air, as if it was attached to a string tugged upwards by some unseen puppeteer.

I stared down at the figure tied to the altar. A vivid cross of red paint marked the spot beneath which his heart lay beating, I was sure, as violently as my own.

My grip tightened on the cruel stone knife, the blade glinting, as the blood-red ruby eyes of the grinning skull bore into mine. Inside my head, the ancient voice rose to a piercing scream.

'Cut out his beating heart – and give it to me!'

Watch out for
RETURN OF THE EMERALD SKULL
in spring 2009.

THE EDGE CHRONICLES

THE QUINT TRILOGY

*Follow the adventures of Quint
in the first age of flight!*

THE CURSE OF THE GLOAMGLOZER

Quint and Maris, daughter of the Most High Academe,
are plunged into a terrifying adventure that takes them
deep into the rock upon which Sanctaphrax is built.
Here they unwittingly invoke an ancient curse . . .

THE WINTER KNIGHTS

Quint is a new student at the Knights Academy,
struggling to survive the icy cold of a never-ending winter,
and the ancient feuds that threaten Sanctaphrax.

CLASH OF THE SKY GALLEONS

Quint finds himself caught up in his father's fight
for revenge against the man who killed his family.
They are drawn into a deadly pursuit, a pursuit that will
ultimately lead to the clash of the great sky galleons.

'The most amazing books ever.'
Ellen, 10

'I hated reading . . . now I'm a reading machine!'
Quinn, 15

THE EDGE CHRONICLES

THE TWIG TRILOGY

*Follow the adventures of Twig
in the first age of flight!*

BEYOND THE DEEPWOODS

Abandoned at birth in the perilous Deepwoods,
Twig does what he has always been warned not to do,
and strays from the path . . .

STORMCHASER

Twig, a young crew-member on the *Stormchaser*
sky ship, risks all to collect valuable stormphrax from
the heart of a Great Storm.

MIDNIGHT OVER SANCTAPHRAX

Far out in open sky, a ferocious storm is brewing.
In its path is the city of Sanctaphrax . . .

'Absolutely brilliant.'
Lin-May, **13**

**'Everything about the Edge
Chronicles is amazing.'**
Cameron, **13**

THE EDGE CHRONICLES

THE ROOK TRILOGY

*Follow the adventures of Rook
in the second age of flight!*

THE LAST OF THE SKY PIRATES

Rook dreams of becoming a librarian knight,
and sets out on a dangerous journey into the Deepwoods
and beyond. When he meets the last sky pirate,
he is thrust into a bold adventure . . .

VOX

Rook becomes involved in the evil scheming of Vox Verlix
– can he stop the Edgeworld falling into total chaos?

FREEGLADER

Undertown is destroyed, and Rook and his
friends travel, with waifs and cloddertrogs, to a new
home in the Free Glades.

'They're the best!!'
Zaffie, 15

'Brilliant illustrations and magical storylines.'
Tom, 14